Maximum Thrust!

With a roar like a thousand giant waterfalls, the space shuttle's massive engines throttled up to full power. Sledgehammer acceleration hit Mark's chest, making him gasp and knocking the air out of his lungs. His body grew heavier and heavier from the tremendous thrust, and within seconds he found it nearly impossible to breathe. He tried to look over at R.J. and Blue, but his sight began to darken and his head pounded. He fought for air, but his chest muscles weren't strong enough to fight the titanic G-forces. A wet liquid sprayed across his face and he realized his nose was spurting blood. He thought he heard R.J. scream and then Blue—but the engine noise made it impossible to tell. Spots appeared before his eyes and the far wall began to fade out. *So this is what it feels like to die,* Mark thought. Seconds later, he passed out.

The Adventures of
Mark Heroic
™

FlashPoint—Book 1

A mysterious madman, code-named *The Seal,* has launched a savage crime wave, and the police are powerless to stop him! Using a super-charged dogcatcher truck, a wild dog pack, and an experimental weapon called the Ion Blaster, Mark, Blue, and R.J. strike back with the strangest crime-fighting tools ever invented.

MegaBlast—Book 2

A space launch turns deadly for Mark, Blue, and R.J. when Red Rot, an international fugitive, hijacks America's newest space shuttle. Using tiny robots, Red Rot transforms all who oppose him into mindless machines! Trapped in space, the boys fight a desperate battle for survival.

CyberDeth—Book 3

The CyberWave, an advanced virtual reality computer, has fallen into the hands of the evil General Deth. Infiltrating a top-secret airbase, Mark, Blue, and R.J. steal the world's fastest jet fighter and track the general to his hidden fortress. But with the CyberWave activated, it's impossible to tell what's real!

The Midas Machine—Book 4

During a science experiment gone wrong, Mark, Blue, and R.J. accidentally create a machine which turns ordinary metal to gold! Abducted by *The Chairman,* the shadowy leader of a multinational corporation, the boys' lives are threatened unless they reveal the device's secret. Once they escape, they discover the Midas Machine has powers the world has never seen.

Earth Station One—Book 5

A Mars lander is off course, heading toward earth! Mark, Blue, and R.J. gain control of it but discover a horrible truth: Dr. Raymond Gunn, a renegade scientist, is using the lander to enrich himself while putting the world in danger. Tracking Dr. Gunn to the Antarctic ice shelf, the boys make a desperate attempt to stop a global catastrophe.

About the Authors

Best-selling author Curtis Taylor has written with U.S. Senator Jake Garn, and Betty J. Eadie. He is also an editor and publisher. He attended Brigham Young University on a track scholarship and graduated with a degree in English. He lives with his wife, Janet, and their six children in Northern California.

Todd Hester spent ten years in the aerospace industry with top-secret clearance and worked on highly classified missile, space, and aircraft programs. He has also written short stories, screenplays, and magazine articles. From Wasco, California, he graduated from Brigham Young University with a degree in engineering.

The Adventures of

Mark Heroic ™

MegaBlast

Curtis Taylor · Todd Hester

GOLD LEAF PRESS

The Adventures of Mark Heroic™
MegaBlast

ISBN 1-882723-51-1

© 1995 by Curtis Taylor and Todd Hester
Printed in the United States

Cover illustration: Roger Loveless
Cover and interior design: Alex Roessler
Art direction: Richard Erickson
Production: Robert Davis

MegaBlast

The Bio-Tel

(front)

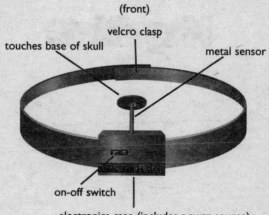

velcro clasp

touches base of skull

metal sensor

on-off switch

electronics case (includes power source)

Monkey Me, Monkey Do

"Grab that chimp before it wrecks the house!" R.J. Rowberry yelled.

Mark Harrison pounded down the stairs after the fleeing chimpanzee. He looked in the living room and saw the chimp crouching behind the couch. Mark smiled—the chimp was smart, but not smart enough. He stalked closer, bent his legs, and lunged.

Mark's arms clutched empty air as the chimp leaped above him. His head slammed into the wall above the couch. The chimp landed on Mark's back, scampered down, then ran into the kitchen, hooting wildly. Mark shook his head to clear his vision. What had started so innocently had turned into a disaster.

The old '50s song "My Blue Heaven" blared from R.J.'s bedroom. Mark and his friend, Blue Berzoni, had gone to R.J.'s house to see if R.J. could make Blue's new boom box play louder.

Mark had even brought one of his mom's Raw Molasses Tofu Cakes to bribe R.J. with. When they got to R.J.'s house, they found a caged chimpanzee in his room. Mark had opened the cage to pet it, and the chimp had bolted.

Footsteps thundered down the stairway as R.J. Rowberry rushed into the living room. His blond flattop, coupled with his Hawaiian shirt and shorts, made quite a sight. Despite weighing at least 250 pounds, R.J. considered himself a body builder and ate only natural foods. The problem was, he ate them by the truck load. But R.J. was also a scientific genius. Except for a few required high school courses, he took all his classes at the National Institute of Technology where his father taught.

R.J. frowned. "Congo's been trying to escape all day. You come over for five minutes and presto, he's gone."

Blue Berzoni, wearing ripped jeans and a Hard Rock Cafe T-shirt bounded down the stairs. His muscles rippled impressively beneath the shirt. Only a sophomore, Blue was the strongest kid in school—and the toughest. It was rumored that Blue had put six gang members in the hospital for offering him drugs. Blue only admitted to trashing two but said it could have been more— math was his worst subject. Blue never picked fights, but he always finished them.

"You're bein' a little hard on him, R.J.," Blue said. "He's only a dumb animal."

"The cage is only for Congo's travel," R.J. protested. "His home at the Vandenberg Animal Research Center is quite spacious."

"I didn't mean Congo," Blue said. "I was talkin' about Harrison. But what can you expect from a guy named Heroic?"

Mark winced. He hated to hear his middle name. His mother had wanted to name him after her brother, Fitzpatrick, but his dad had wanted to give him a more heroic name. Confused by their arguments in the hospital, the nurse had written Heroic on the birth certificate. By the time anyone had noticed, the name was registered. At only five eight and 140 pounds, though, Mark felt anything but heroic. He was good at schoolwork, but average at everything else—except making himself look stupid.

Loud smacking noises came from the kitchen. "Not the cake!" R.J. yelled.

The three boys charged down the hallway and found Congo sitting on the kitchen table, stuffing a handful of tofu cake into his mouth. Cheeks bulging, the animal looked more like a huge chipmunk than a chimpanzee.

"That's R.J.'s!" Mark yelled. He dove across the table, but Congo jumped onto the overhead chandelier. Mark skidded off the table and crashed to the floor.

"I'll get him!" Blue said, rushing forward. His right arm shot up toward the chimp, but Congo leaped into the air, making the light fixture swing. Blue's hand accidentally hit the chandelier and knocked it out of the ceiling in a shower of broken plaster. Congo landed on the refrigerator, still holding his handful of cake. With his other hand, he grabbed an apple from a fruit bowl and beaned R.J. on the head.

"Ow!" R.J. bellowed. "Nobody steals my cake!" He threw his huge body forward, leaping as high as he could. Soaring three inches above the floor, R.J. hit the refrigerator door and popped it open. He bounced back and grabbed the open door for balance, tilting the fridge toward him. An avalanche of Jell-O, gravy, and mashed potatoes cascaded onto his head.

Congo bounded to the microwave and popped the cake into his mouth. Then he vaulted to the floor and dashed away.

R.J. scooped the leftovers off his head. "My father is going to kill me." He looked at the mixed leftovers in his hand then slopped some into his mouth. "Mmm, not bad."

"How are we gonna catch him?" Blue asked, laying the broken chandelier on the table. "He's too fast."

R.J. stood up, wiping his head with a towel. "I

don't know, but we must do it immediately. Scientists from Vandenberg Air Base will be here any minute to pick him up. My father was going to take Congo to the base today, but he got called to the Pentagon." R.J. paused dramatically. "Dire situations call for dire measures. Please, follow me."

Mark and Blue followed R.J. up to his bedroom. The room was packed with computers, electronic components, and chemistry equipment. "My Blue Heaven" had finished on Blue's boom box and "Blue Monday" was halfway through. R.J. clicked off the unit and turned to Blue. "Are you sure you want me to make it louder? It's quite annoying, already."

"All your songs are really old, too," Mark complained. "Don't you have anything newer?"

"Naw, I only buy songs with my name in 'em," Blue said. "Things like 'Love Is Blue,' 'Blue Velvet,' 'Blue Lagoon,' 'Blue Moon,' 'Blue . . .'"

"Enough!" R.J. interrupted, "Don't you have any headphones?"

Blue shrugged. "Sure. I didn't know you hated good music." He pulled a small, plastic case from his back pocket and removed a pair of headphones.

"Don't put them on now," R.J. said. "I have something to show you."

"Make up your mind," Blue said. He put the headphones back into the case and sat it on top of R.J.'s desk.

R.J. went to his closet, changed shirts, then came back and pulled another plastic case from his middle desk drawer. "This will allow Mark to capture Congo."

Blue gazed at it. "Is that somethin' to make Harrison smarter?"

"Unfortunately, no," R.J. said. "That is beyond the power of science. This case contains several BioBot Telemetry Units. I call them BioTels for short. Each BioTel works with a device called a BioBot. My father invented BioBots after the *Challenger* shuttle disaster in Florida. His purpose was to replace human astronauts with chimpanzees. They're highly classified, of course. My father's a brilliant scientist, but not very good at keeping secrets."

"How do they work?" Mark asked.

"BioBot stands for *Biological Robot*," R.J. explained. "It's a microscopic radio transmitter combined with a miniature computer. It travels into a chimp's brain through its bloodstream. There it intercepts what the chimp sees, hears and feels and transmits it to the BioTel. A human controller wearing the BioTel receives the impulses, thereby seeing what the chimp sees, hearing what it hears, and feeling what it feels."

"It's like being inside the chimp," Mark said.

"Precisely," R.J. acknowledged. "But that's not the best part. When the human controller tries to move, the BioTel will intercept the human's movement command and send it to the chimp's BioBot instead, making the chimp move. So, for example, when the human moves his hand, the chimp's hand will move instead. The human will see through the chimp's eyes, and the chimp will move as if it were the human. People on earth will be able to perform dangerous tasks in space through the bodies of chimps."

"That's unbelievable!" Mark said.

"No, that's science," R.J. corrected. "Congo will be piloting the shuttle *Explorer* into space tomorrow. Or rather, Colonel Boggs, the shuttle pilot, will be piloting the shuttle through Congo. That's why Congo's being picked up. This is the first shuttle mission using the BioBot system. From now on, space travel will be perfectly safe."

"Except for Congo," Blue said. "I bet nobody asked him."

R.J. ignored Blue's comment. "We will now get a preview of the BioBot system," R.J. said. "Through Mark."

"What?" Mark asked, surprised.

R.J. took one of the BioTels out of the case and handed it to Mark. "You let Congo out of his cage, therefore you will put on a BioTel and bring him back."

Mark looked at the device. "Is it safe?"

"Theoretically, yes," R.J. said, "but be careful. The BioTels in this case are untested."

Mark studied the device, which appeared to be a strap of flat, nylon cord fitted into a loop with a dime-sized metal sensor on back. A credit-card sized electronics module protruded from one side. R.J. slipped the loop over Mark's head and down around his neck. Then he tightened it until the metal sensor in back contacted the base of his skull.

"Now what?" Mark asked.

"Just press the button on back," R.J. said.

Mark reached behind his neck and pressed the button. Instantly his vision blurred. When his sight cleared he saw that he wasn't in R.J.'s room anymore but was in the kitchen. His nose itched, and he brought his hand up to scratch it.

He screamed as he saw a hairy arm reaching for his throat! Congo was attacking! Mark leaped off the kitchen table, turned to run, then saw a shaggy figure in the hallway mirror—he was looking at a reflection of Congo! The hairy arm he'd seen reaching for his throat was his own! Mark looked in the mirror, transfixed. He lifted his right arm, and the chimp did also. Then he jumped into the air and saw Congo make the same move.

Mark leaped up to the brass light fixture in the entry way, grabbed it with both hands, then hung upside down. It was incredible! The BioBot actually worked. He was inside Congo's body!

"Mark!" R.J. bellowed from above. "Get up here!"

Mark dropped to the floor, dashed up the stairs, ran into R.J.'s room and slipped into Congo's cage. R.J. shut and locked it.

Inside the cage now, Mark watched a skinny kid get off the bed and scratch his armpits. Then the kid put his knuckles on the floor and walked across the room like a monkey.

Blue laughed. "That's pretty funny, Harrison!"

He was that skinny kid, Mark suddenly realized. Congo was inside his body—just as *he* was inside Congo's. They had traded places. R.J. hadn't said anything about that. Fascinated, Mark watched as his body got back on the bed and jumped up and down. A small, black beetle suddenly skittered across the floor. Mark saw himself pounce on it, pop it into his mouth and chew rapidly.

"That ruled, Harrison!" Blue laughed. "You're finally actin' like a man."

"That's enough," R.J. said. He turned off the BioTel.

Mark's vision blurred, and when his eyes

refocused, he found himself standing between his two friends. Congo was in the cage. Mark was back in his own body, but there was a strange taste in his mouth—the beetle! He spit out the insect and wiped his tongue frantically on his shirt. "Congo was inside me! He made me eat a bug!"

"Got any tarantulas?" Blue asked R.J. "Looks like Harrison missed lunch."

"Forget it," Mark said. "I think I'm going to barf."

"You're actin' like a wimp," Blue said flatly. "I liked you better as a monkey. Put the BioBarf back on."

"It's called a BioTel, not a BioBarf," R.J. said severely. He laid the BioTel next to its plastic case. "The two-way personality switch is quite unexpected. I'll have to remember to mention it to Colonel Boggs before he tests it."

Mark felt sick. "I think I need my stomach pumped. You'd better call 9-1-1." He bent over.

Blue went to the phone. "What's the number?"

R.J. rolled his eyes. "You don't know the phone number for 9-1-1?"

"Never mind," Blue said. "I'll get it from the operator." He thought for a moment. "What's the operator's number?"

The doorbell rang.

"That's probably the two scientists," R.J. said. "Mark, help me get Congo downstairs." R.J. and Mark picked up Congo's wire cage and held it between them. "Blue, you put the BioTel in its case and bring it downstairs."

"I thought Lincoln freed the slaves," Blue grumbled. Nevertheless, he put the device into its plastic case and started for the door. "Hold on," he said. "I better grab my headphones, too." He grabbed the case they were in, rushed toward the door, and stumbled over a coiled extension cord. The two cases fell to the floor.

"That's my Harrison imitation," Blue said. "Have feet, will trip." He stuffed one of the small cases into his back pocket and grabbed the other.

They hurried downstairs. Two men in dark suits entered when R.J. opened the door. A tall, muscular man with bushy hair stood in front. He had a hooked nose and dense sloping shoulders. The other man stood behind him. He was short and wiry with an angry red scar across his cheek.

"We're here for Congo," the big man said.

"Colonel Boggs sent us," his companion agreed.

R.J. nodded. "I was expecting you." He held out the cage and the big man took it. "Don't forget the BioTels," R.J. added.

Blue handed the plastic case to the other man.

The two men left the porch, got into a brown sedan, and drove off.

The phone rang and R.J. went to get it. "Hello, Colonel Boggs," he said a moment later. "No, this is R.J. My father's been called to the Pentagon, but everything's under control. Your men already picked up Congo and the BioTels." R.J. listened again and a shocked expression came over his face. "You can't mean that?" he said. "I had no way of knowing. Of course I'll come immediately to Vandenberg and look at mug shots—I'm sure I can identify them. Yes, I can stay the weekend if need be. I'll leave within the hour." R.J. hung the phone up, a dazed look on his face. "Blue, can you and Mark drive me to Vandenberg now? It's an emergency."

Blue thought for a moment. "I guess so. My sister and brother-in-law are visitin' my cousin Nikki in L.A. They won't be back till Monday. We can take Allie's dog-catcher truck."

Mark wondered what the problem was. "I'll have to ask my parents," he said, "but I'm sure it'll be okay. What's the emergency?"

R.J. took a deep breath and tried to calm himself. "Those two men were impostors! Congo's been kidnaped!"

Comic Relief

Blue skidded the dog truck to a stop in front of Mark's house on Cypress Avenue. Mark had tried to call but the phone had been busy.

"You sure Allie won't mind us taking the dog truck to Vandenberg for the weekend?" Mark asked, getting out. "You just got your license back and the truck is city property." Blue's sister, Allie, was the Saint Clare dogcatcher.

"I told ya she's gone till Monday," Blue said. "She ain't gonna mind, 'cause she ain't gonna know. Tell your mom you're goin'. I'll get some gas and be back in a half hour." Mark hopped out and Blue sped away.

Mark jogged up the walk and opened the door. He sniffed the air for any scent of his mother's cooking. Mark had had a heart murmur as a young child, and the doctor had ordered his mother to cook only special health foods. Mark got over the heart problem long ago, but his mom never got over cooking health food. Now, every meal was an adventure, usually with a bad ending. Mark decided it was safe. "Hi, Mom! I'm home!"

A small head suddenly popped up from behind the living room couch. "Die, scum!" a high-pitched voice yelled.

Before Mark could react, three white spit wads shot out of a Burger World straw, streaked across the room, and splattered against his cheek.

"That's it, Clint!" Mark yelled. "I warned you about those . . ."

His mother came around the corner. "I thought I heard you."

Clint, Mark's younger brother, quickly whipped the straw behind his back. "Mark's yellin' at me."

His mother shook her head. "Honestly, Mark. Try to be more mature than a ten-year-old."

Mark took a deep breath. It wouldn't do any good to accuse Clint. His little brother was so sneaky he could hide evidence from Sherlock Holmes. "Can I spend the night with R.J. at the . . . ?"

"What a wonderful idea," his mother said. "It's going to be hectic enough around here tonight as it is. Clint's Cub Scout pack is having a backyard sleep over." She glanced at her watch. "Got to run, now. I've got a five o'clock PTA meeting. Clint, get in the car."

Clint rushed to her side, then stuck his tongue out at Mark.

"Have fun, Mark." She paused and looked back. "Did R.J. enjoy the cake I made?"

"Didn't monkey around with it a bit," Mark said truthfully. "Every crumb got eaten."

His mother nodded. "R.J. is so sensible in his choice of foods. Bye, dear." She rushed out, shutting the door behind her.

Mark went to his room, grabbed a duffel bag, and stuffed in an extra change of clothes. He looked out the window. Blue wasn't back yet, so Mark opened his bottom dresser drawer and pulled out a shoe box labeled "Secret Junk-Food Stash." He opened the lid and looked inside.

A small note lay on top: "Dear Mark, I threw away your candy and replaced it with Honey Lentil Soy Muffins. They're much better for you. Love, Mom." Four of the horrible, brown creations sat inside.

Mark carefully replaced the lid and chuckled deviously. Just as he had planned. He'd thrown his mother off his trail once again. He quickly crossed the room, reached under his bed, and slid out his real, secret junk food box. Mark kept the contraband hidden in a granola box. Even if his mom noticed the box, she'd figure that it was something healthy. Mark unwrapped a Ding

Dong, powered it down in two bites, then grabbed a bag of nacho cheese tortilla chips.

Savage, high-pitched barks came from the back yard, startling Mark. With the ease of experience, he whipped the contraband back into the granola box and stuffed it under his bed. He listened carefully, afraid his mother had doubled back through the alley. She could be sneaky sometimes. But there were no more noises. It was probably just his five-pound killer poodle, Miss Fluffy. She liked to terrorize Rasputin, the German shepherd next door. Miss Fluffy had been raised by a family of pit bulls and was unbeatable in a fight. Even though it was a false alarm, Mark left the granola box where it was. He really wasn't hungry.

Blue still wasn't back, so Mark reached into the headboard of his bed and got his favorite comic book, *Destructo the Monster-Tamer*, Issue Number One. To Mark, this book deserved recognition as a modern literary classic. Never mind what his teachers said about Steinbeck, Hemingway, and Shakespeare; he'd take Destructo any day. Mark read at least one of his Destructo comics every day. He prided himself on being the world's foremost Destructo expert. He opened it.

Flame Finger, the greatest of all cosmic criminals, had trapped Destructo in a gravity-grip. He gloated over his seeming victory. "So, Super Hero, you had thought to capture me, but it is I who have captured you. I will now burn you into galactic oblivion with my finger of flame!"

Mark's mind wandered back to R.J.'s house. It was strange that someone would kidnap a chimpanzee. You certainly couldn't ask for a ransom from the chimp's family. What could they offer? A hundred pounds of bananas? No, there had to be a deeper reason. Something to do with the space shuttle perhaps? Mark didn't know. But whatever it was, Mark was sure the Air Force would get to the bottom of it. He looked back at the page.

Destructo stared fearlessly into the eyes of the evil mastermind. "You have conquered nothing. I allowed myself to be captured so I would be brought to you." His Justice Stone glowed bright red. "As long as I am pure of heart and mind, I am invincible!" With a burst of mighty power, Destructo shattered his bonds. Cowed by the uncovered wrath of Destructo, Flame-Finger slunk back.

"Good ol' Destructo," Mark mumbled, "we could sure use you now. You'd have Congo back quicker than . . ."

The doorbell broke into his thoughts. Mark threw down the comic, grabbed his duffel bag, and r an to the front door.

"What took you so long, Harrison?" Blue said. "I been ringin' the bell for five minutes. I woulda just came in except I was afraid your mom might be cookin' something. We were supposed to pick up R.J. ten minutes ago."

"Sorry," Mark said, coming out and shutting the door behind him. "I got carried away with my Destructo comic."

Blue rolled his eyes. "You're always readin', man. The only readin' I do is at gunpoint. Books don't do ya any good."

"Books are full of imagination," Mark said, "and imagination is the keystone of creativity. Creativity is very important."

"Sounds like somethin' Mister Rogers would say." Blue jumped into the driver's seat and mimicked Mr. Rogers' voice: "Can you spell *wimp*, boys and girls?"

Mark shrugged and hoped Blue didn't notice that he was blushing. He *had* heard Mister Rogers talk about imagination years ago. Mark decided to remain quiet.

"I'm actually lookin' forward to this," Blue

said. "I ain't had a vacation since I got suspended from school for two days last week. I need a break."

Mark nodded. Congo's abduction was probably just a mistake. After R.J. cleared that up, they'd have the whole weekend free on the coast. Mark smiled to himself. The next few days were going to be nothing but fun.

Red Rot

She was breathtaking.

Standing eleven stories high and weighing four and a-half-million pounds, the Space Shuttle *Explorer* stood ready for launch at California's Vandenberg Air Force Base. Fuel lines ran from the gantry standing next to it to the spacecraft's external tank, which fed the *Explorer's* three internal engines. The tank, half as long as a football field, held enough fuel to fill 135 swimming pools. The *Explorer's* engines put out enough force to equal one quarter of the power released by the Hiroshima atomic bomb. Going from zero to Mach 1 in only fifty seconds, the *Explorer* was a true wonder of the world.

Five miles away, a semi-truck turned off the main highway and rumbled toward the Vandenberg delivery gate. A Farm Fresh Foods sign had been painted on its side. The driver and his female passenger stared at the distant space-craft.

"Hard to believe something that big can get off the ground, Gov'nuh," the woman said. She took a large knitting needle and a small plastic case from her handbag. She opened the case, pulled out a small dart, and slipped it into the hollow needle. "I just hope these BioBots work," she said. "I don't want to anger Nimrod."

"Don't fret, old girl," the man answered. "With Nimrod on the inside, we've got nothing to worry about. The microscopic biological robots loaded in those hypodermic darts are in perfect working order—as is this BioBot Voice Control Unit." He took out a flat metal case from the glove box and slipped it into his front pocket. Then he plugged a small microphone jack into the metal case and clipped the microphone onto his collar. It was barely visible.

"Can Nimrod hear us now?" the woman asked.

"Nimrod is always with us," the man said. "Who would have thought that I, Sir Redford Rottingham, also known as Red Rot, and you, Minerva Minnifield, alias the Nanny, would be in the employ of a criminal mastermind like Nimrod. After all, everyone thinks we're criminal masterminds, ourselves."

"Yes, Gov'nuh, I dare say we make quite a pair." Her dry lips almost smiled. "And if the

BioBots work as well as they have in the past, stealing the *Explorer* should be a breeze."

Red Rot slowed the truck as they approached the gate.

Airman First Class Edgar Benson sat in the guard booth at the Vandenberg delivery gate. Listening to a Friday night baseball game, he was oblivious to the sound of the Farm Fresh Truck pulling up to his window. A former high school shortstop from Chicago, Illinois, he was more concerned that his beloved Cubs were two runs down to the Dodgers. An English accent from outside the booth jerked him back from Wrigley Field.

"Pardon me, old chap, but is this the gate for cafeteria deliveries?"

Benson turned down the game. A thin man in his middle fifties sat in the cab of the familiar semi. Benson nodded and opened the booth's sliding window. The man handed him a photo gate pass.

The picture matched the driver's face, but the man's neatly trimmed mustache and perfectly manicured hands seemed at odds with his grubby coveralls. Suddenly, Benson didn't care that Cubs' cleanup hitter, Vinnie 'Hot' Pantz, was coming up with the bases loaded. Something was wrong. He turned off the radio.

"Joe sick tonight . . . Bubba?" Benson asked, reading the driver's name off the pass.

The driver smiled. "Yes, I'm afraid he is."

Benson knew he was lying. The regular driver's name wasn't Joe.

An older woman leaned over from the passenger's seat. She was dressed in a drab, woolen skirt and a plain, white blouse. Her brown hair, streaked with gray, was pulled back in a bun. Fine lines crinkled her face. But what struck Benson were her eyes—dark, piercing, and somehow desperate. "Joe's got a touch of the flu," she said with a Cockney twang.

Despite the warm evening air, Benson shivered. Trying to act normal, he reached for his rifle.

Behind the semi, an old pickup turned off the main road and pulled to a stop behind the big rig.

The woman frowned at Benson. "You're holding up traffic, Mate."

"Just let me log you in." Benson said. He grabbed his AR-15 assault rifle and jammed it into the driver's face. "Freeze! Frankie's the regular driver, not Joe! Who are you?"

"Easy, old chap," the driver said, raising his hands. "Joe's a real person. He's Frankie's normal replacement. But he's sick tonight also. I'm replacing the replacement, so to speak."

Benson didn't relax. The explanation seemed too convenient. He pointed the assault rifle at the woman. "Let's see your I.D."

"Of course, Dearie," the woman said. She reached into a large handbag. "It's here some-where." She moved a ball of yarn to the side, jerked a knitting needle to her lips, and puffed sharply.

Benson saw the movement but dodged too slowly. A dart flew from the needle and stuck in his neck. He brought the rifle to his shoulder to fire.

The driver spoke into his collar microphone. "Don't shoot."

Benson's finger eased off the trigger. He wanted to fire, but he couldn't force his finger to move. Mustering his last bit of fading will, he reached toward the Emergency Alert button on the inside console.

"Don't touch anything!" the driver ordered. "Drop your hands."

Under Red Rot's complete control now, Benson obeyed.

Red Rot spoke again. "Get General Robbins, the new base commander, out here. And call my old friend Colonel Boggs, too. Tell them it's an emergency." Red Rot smiled humorlessly at the Nanny. "So the game begins."

Assault and Pepper

Singing along with Elvis Presley's "Blue Suede Shoes" on his boom box, Blue drove down the two-lane road toward Vandenberg's delivery gate. R.J. sat next to the window with his eyes closed and fingers in his ears.

In the middle, Mark glanced at a small switch under the dash. Some time ago they had secretly installed a nitrous oxide injector in the engine. A flip of that switch transformed the broken-down dog truck into a 150-mile-per-hour dragster. Because of the danger of blowing the engine, they rarely used it. Blue's sister had never noticed it.

Blue hit an off-key note that rattled Mark's teeth. "Can't you turn that off for a while?" Mark asked, his ears ringing. "At least put on your headphones."

Blue looked over. "No way, Man. I can't find my phones and I love this song. It's got my name in it." He started singing again, twice as loud.

Mark turned and stared out the window. He should be angry, but he was only annoyed. He didn't get mad easily. Mark tried to overlook people's faults and concentrate on their good qualities. With Blue, however, he had to try a little harder.

They crested a hill, and Vandenberg Air Force Base opened beneath them. The *Explorer* loomed large in the distance. As the sun slowly set behind the sand dunes to the west, the massive ship became illuminated in spotlights. Ignoring Blue's protest, Mark shut off the tape and nudged R.J. in the side. "Check it out. I didn't think it was so big."

R.J. opened his eyes and leaned forward in the seat. "Quite impressive."

"Not really," Blue said, closing one eye and sighting along his hand. "It's only as big as my thumb."

"Which is still larger than your brain," R.J. said. "The *Explorer* looks small because it's so far away. Distance makes all objects appear smaller."

"Maybe," Blue said. "But I bet from far away you still look as big as a house."

"We're coming to the turnoff," Mark interrupted. "Don't miss it."

Following the signs, Blue drove down the hill and through the security fence. A big rig truck was stopped at the security booth, its driver talking to an Air Force guard.

Blue flashed his lights and honked his horn, but the big rig didn't move.

"Wait here, Blue," R.J. said, impatiently. "Mark and I will phone Colonel Boggs from the guardhouse."

Mark and R.J. got out of the truck. Blue yawned and lay down in the front seat.

As Mark and R.J. approached the gate, a man and woman got out of the truck.

"The base is closed for the night," the man said.

"That's right, lads," the woman said. "We're the last truck they're letting in."

"But I have an appointment," R.J. complained. He turned to the guard, who had remained strangely silent. "I need to call Colonel Pepper Boggs."

Headlights appeared in the darkness, and a Humvee military vehicle motored toward them.

"You're in luck, lad," the driver said. "That should be Colonel Boggs and General Robbins now." He nodded to the woman, and they stepped behind the big rig.

Mark had an uneasy feeling. "Why's a general coming to the delivery gate?" he whispered to R.J. "Something's wrong."

"Nothing's wrong," R.J. said. "Congo is very important. They were probably coming to wait for us to arrive."

The Humvee stopped by the booth, and a stern-faced man in a decorated general's uniform got out. Mark assumed it was General Robbins. The general's weathered face showed the marks of military campaigns in harsh climates, but his posture was straight and his movements forceful and strong.

"What's the meaning of this, soldier?" Robbins yelled, stopping in front of the guard. "We're in the middle of a kidnaping investigation. Can't you check in two vehicles without calling me? I see no security alert here." He motioned to a man in the Humvee. "Get over here, Boggs."

Colonel Boggs got out and walked over. He was shorter than the general, but his jutting jaw and barrel chest made him seem larger. Though his deliberate stride hinted at stern self-control, his eyes had a friendly twinkle. Deep laugh lines creased the corners of his mouth.

"Now, General, sir," Boggs said in a southern drawl, "Benson's a good man. I promoted him myself. I'm sure he had a good reason to call." He looked into Benson's impassive face. "I hope you weren't just lonely, airman."

Before Benson could answer, R.J. stepped forward. "Excuse me, sir. But I'm Professor Rowberry's son, R.J. I talked to you on the phone about Congo."

Boggs sighed deeply. "Thank goodness you made it. I thought you had forgotten. If we don't get Congo back soon , the shuttle launch will be canceled."

General Robbins turned to the guard. "My apology, Airman Benson. Instead of a reprimand, I might give you a promotion. We've been waiting for this young man."

Benson tilted his head toward the big rig. "*He* told me to call you."

The man and woman stepped into the open. For the first time, Mark noticed a small microphone clipped to the man's shirt collar.

"A truck driver told you to call me?" General Robbins sputtered. "By what authority?"

The man reached into his coveralls and pulled out a pistol. "By this authority."

Mark and R.J. were shocked into silence.

"Wha . . . what's going on here?" General Robbins stammered.

Colonel Boggs turned to the guard. "He's armed! Do something!"

Benson didn't move.

"Don't just stand there!" the general ordered. "Call for reinforcements!"

The woman reached into a large handbag, pulled out another pistol, and held it to Robbins' head. "Quiet." She turned to Boggs. "Tell the general who he's dealing with, Colonel."

Boggs studied their faces then spoke in disbelief. "Red Rot and the Nanny?" A shocked expression crossed his face. "But you were both sentenced to life in prison!" He stared at Red Rot's collar. "You've got a BioVoice—and you've injected the guard with a BioBot!"

"What's going on, Boggs?" General Robbins demanded. "What are BioVoices and BioBots? Who are these people?"

"Sir Redford Rottingham and Mrs. Minerva Minnifield, sir," Boggs said hoarsely. "Formerly they were the top agents for MI-5, the British Secret Service. They were convicted last year of trying to steal classified mind-control devices called BioBots. The microphone on Red Rot's collar controls the BioBots—it's called a BioVoice. I captured these two myself, before you were transferred here, and the Brits locked them up in Parkhurst Prison on the Isle of Wight."

A slight smile played on the Nanny's face. "The damp weather didn't agree with us, Colonel. So we decided to take a holiday in sunny California."

Red Rot nodded. "What you didn't know when you caught us was that I had already stolen a box of BioBots and a BioVoice. If I'd had them when we were arrested, I'd never have been captured. When I finally had them smuggled into prison, escape was easy."

Mark glanced at R.J. He appeared to be petrified.

"What are you doing here?" the general asked.

"We're stealing the space shuttle," Red Rot said. He turned to the Nanny. "Dart him."

She brought the knitting needle to her lips and puffed.

The general slapped his neck and pulled out a small dart. "I'll have you arrested for assault and . . ." His eyes glazed over and his words drifted off.

"Close the base, General," Red Rot spoke into the BioVoice, "and confine all personnel to their quarters. All further orders will come through me. My squad will run the Command Bunker."

The general nodded. "You are in control." He went inside the guard booth, picked up a phone, and began talking.

Red Rot pounded on the trailer. "Leonard! Pope! Get the squad out here!"

The trailer door opened and twenty armed men, dressed in black combat fatigues, rushed out.

A bushy-haired man with bulging muscles stepped up to Red Rot. "It's about time something happened. If I were in charge, I'd . . ."

"I don't want to hear it, Pope," Red Rot said.

"You're nothing but hired help."

A man with a scarred face stepped up boldly. "Don't talk to Pope like that. He was the chief ground controller at the Johnson Space Center for years—until we got fired because of budget cuts, that is. Show some respect. We didn't take this job to be yelled at by some namby-pamby British dandy."

"Correct, Leonard," Red Rot said. "You came here to follow my orders. So do what I say and shut up!"

Leonard tensed, took a step toward the Englishman, and tried to shove him. The Nanny stepped forward quickly, grabbed Leonard's wrist, and twisted it savagely. He tried to shake free but she pressed her forearm against his elbow and forced him painfully to the ground.

"Should I break it?" The Nanny asked, her eyes flashing like black diamonds.

Leonard met her gaze for a moment, then shook his head, beads of sweat rolling down his forehead. "I give! I give!"

"Wise," Red Rot said. "She's a jiu-jitsu black belt." He nodded at the Nanny. "Let him up."

The Nanny let go, and Leonard got up, flexing his sore arm.

Mark looked at Pope and Leonard carefully. "You're the two men who kidnaped Congo and stole the BioTels!"

"You've got Congo, too?" Boggs thundered. "That chimp is the property of the U.S. Air Force!"

Red Rot smiled. "He's my property now, Colonel." He looked at his two men. "Take General Robbins and the guard to the Command Bunker. The Nanny and I will follow you in the general's Humvee."

Pope and Leonard got in front. The other hired men took General Robbins and the guard to the back of the Farm Fresh truck. Moments later it rumbled off toward the Command Bunker.

"Shall I dart Boggs?" the Nanny asked.

"No," Red Rot said. "We need him to control Congo and fly the shuttle. The BioBot will control his mind, but dull his wits. We'll take him with us to the Command Bunker."

"How about these two lads?"

Red Rot shrugged. "We have a limited supply of BioBots, and I don't think Nimrod has any use for them. Kill them."

Blue Suede Shoes

Boggs started to drop his head in defeat then suddenly leaped forward in a cross-body block, slamming Red Rot and the Nanny to the ground. "Run, boys!"

Mark and Blue sprinted toward the dog truck. "Start the truck, Blue!" Mark yelled.

The truck's high beams suddenly split the night as its engine roared on. Blue hit the accelerator, and a plume of dirt spun off the truck's rear wheels. Blue had triggered the injector!

Boggs untangled himself from the two hijackers and rushed after the boys. Mark and R.J. jumped out of the way as the dog truck flashed by, aiming for the two criminals. Red Rot and the Nanny dove inside the guard booth, firing recklessly into the blinding headlights. Mark hoped Blue had enough sense to keep his head down.

The dog truck sped on, a rain of bullets

sparking off its hood and grill. Red Rot and the Nanny dove out the back window of the guard booth just as Blue plowed in through the front. Shattered glass exploded through the air, and chunks of wood rained everywhere. Blue slammed the truck into reverse and pulled away from the flattened structure.

The engine revved again, and the dog truck spun around in a short arc, its rear wheels pointing at the ruined booth. Red Rot and the Nanny charged out of the darkness through the debris, firing as they advanced.

Blue took the truck out of gear and mashed the accelerator. The engine screamed higher and higher until it seemed it might explode. Then Blue slapped the truck into first and popped the clutch. The rear wheels spun out, sending a stream of dirt and gravel backwards that hit Red Rot and the Nanny like water from a fire hose, lifting them off their feet and throwing them backwards. The wheels caught, and the truck powered down the road.

Blue skidded to a stop beside Mark, R.J., and Boggs. "Get in!" he yelled.

Mark and Boggs dove through the passengers' door, and R.J. scrambled in back.

"We're outta here!" Blue yelled over the engine. He floored the gas pedal and headed for the exit.

"No!" Boggs screamed. "The general closed the base. All the gates shut automatically!"

The headlights reflected off a sliding chain-link gate that now blocked the road.

"I'll ram it!" Blue yelled.

"No!" Boggs screamed. "It's electrified with one million volts!"

Blue stomped on the brake with both feet, flinging everyone forward. The truck fishtailed toward the fence, and Blue wrestled with the wheel, fighting to keep the truck from spinning out of control. Five feet from the fence the truck finally shuddered to a stop. Dust swirled around them, a thick layer settling in the cab.

"Now what?" Blue choked through the dust. "We're dead meat here."

R.J. pounded on the cab window and pointed back. Mark turned around and opened the access window to the cage.

"More Humvees!" R.J. yelled through the small window. Mark looked past R.J. and saw five sets of headlights approaching.

"Red Rot must have had General Robbins radio for help," Boggs said. He thought for a moment. "Listen, there's a tunnel a few miles north, just beyond a dry ravine. It's part of the Vandenberg water system. It's big enough to hide the truck in—if we can make it."

Blue backed up the truck, turned the wheel

left, and bumped over the dirt berm that lined the road. He flipped off the injector. "Can't drive fast in this stuff, anyway."

The open range was an obstacle course of waist-high brush, hidden ruts, and dry gulches. Blue wove through as fast as possible, but the terrain was too rough for the truck to make good time. Behind, in the truck bed, R.J. groaned with every bump.

Colonel Boggs looked out the window. "The Humvees are gaining and we're still a mile from the cave. Quit weaving and go straight."

"I can't," Blue said. "I'll hit something and smash the radiator."

The Humvees had already halved the gap between them, Mark saw. At this rate they'd be caught in a few minutes. Mark had a thought. "Blue, aren't you good at driving backwards?"

"A pro," Blue said, weaving the truck between bushes. "I started backin' my sister's car down the driveway when I was nine, but I only got my driver's license last year. So I got one year of experience drivin' forward, and eight years goin' backwards."

"Then drive backwards," Mark said. "It'll protect the radiator from the bushes and let you go straighter. We'll make better time."

Blue slammed on the brakes and began turning.

"It's useless!" R.J. yelled through the glass. "The Humvees have higher ground clearance and are going forward. They'll be on us in no time!"

"I plan to buy us some time," Mark said. He grabbed the dog truck's C.B. radio mike and turned it on.

"You'll never reach anyone on the radio!" Boggs said. "We're miles from any police station. Plus, those Hummer's have full-range scanners. Red Rot's men will hear everything you say!"

"That's what I'm counting on," Mark said. He keyed the handset to transmit. "Attention police! Attention police! This is a civilian, uh, dog truck, and we're being chased by a squad of Humvees at Vandenberg Air Base. We have no hope of escape so we plan to ram our pursuers. We've rigged our gas tank to explode and are going to take as many of them with us as we can! If you can hear us, please send medical crews immediately!"

"Brilliant, Mark!" R.J. exclaimed.

Blue threw the truck into reverse and backed up. The Humvees behind them slowed, then stopped.

"It worked!" Boggs said. "They see our headlights and think we're going to ram them!"

Blue looked into the side mirror. "I see the ravine!" he said. "We're going to make it!"

Suddenly, though, he slammed on the brakes.

Mark heard a thump as R.J. slid across the floor and hit against the back gate. "What are you doing?" R.J. screamed.

"I hear water!" Blue yelled. "Something's wrong!"

Mark and Boggs rushed out of the truck to the embankment. Blue came up behind them. A raging sheet of white water, twenty feet across, pounded through the bottom of a deep ravine.

"It must have rained in the mountains," Boggs said. "It's a flash flood! We can't cross!"

They ran back to the dog truck just as the radio crackled to life. "This is Red Rot in Humvee One! Boggs and the kids tricked us. They're not ramming us, they're driving backwards. All units advance!"

Blue started the dog truck and drove toward the advancing Humvees.

"What are you doing?" R.J. yelled from the back. "Ramming them was just a trick! Mark didn't mean it!"

Blue suddenly spun the truck back toward the flooded gulch. "I ain't gonna ram 'em! I'm gonna get us across that ravine. Fasten your seat belts, we're gonna catch some air." He put on his shoulder harness. "I just hope we can get off the ground with Fatberry in back."

Boggs' face turned white. "You're not thinking

of jumping the ravine? I know a place downstream where we can cross."

"Too late," Blue said. "Hang on." He put his hand on the gearshift and gunned the engine.

R.J. pounded on the window. "Let me out!"

Mark glanced behind. The Humvees were only a hundred yards behind. Automatic rifles chattered, and white muzzle flashes lit the night. "They're shooting! Jump on it!"

Blue flipped the injector switch, and the engine thundered into a deafening roar. Blue shifted into first and hit the gas. The truck leaped into a wheelie, pinning Mark and Boggs against the seat. R.J. flattened himself on the floor in back as the truck jarred forward.

"Get ready for takeoff!" Blue yelled. "Thanks for flyin' Air Berzoni!"

The jarring suddenly stopped. Mark looked out the window and saw water below. They were airborne.

Dark Secrets

The truck smashed into the ground, and the rear end tilted up. The truck started to cartwheel then the bumper gave way and the truck spurted forward. The rear wheels banged onto the ground, bounced, then hit again and settled down. Blue flipped the injector off and guided the truck to a stop.

Mark spun around and looked out the back window. The Humvees hadn't seen the ravine in time, and now two of them rested halfway down the embankment on their sides, and another one lay upside down in the roaring flood. Three men floundered in the water, holding onto their vehicle. Pope and Leonard got out of their Humvee, scrambled to a ledge halfway down to the water, and threw out rescue lines.

Blue's arm had hit the steering wheel but didn't look broken. Mark's back hurt, and Boggs held his neck and moaned. In back, R.J. had managed to hold onto the floor. He was so well padded that

Mark figured he had fared the best. All that really mattered, though, was they were still alive.

"Jumpin' stuff in cars looks a lot easier on TV," Blue groaned. "I think I sprained my wrist." He looked down at the floor and groaned loudly. "Not my boom box!" The unit was a mass of broken plastic and twisted wires.

"Forget your boom box," R.J. said, rubbing his rear. "I think I sprained my . . ."

"Listen!" Boggs interrupted. "Air patrol!"

Helicopter blades churned in the distance. Blue looked out his window. "Three searchlights are comin' outta the sky."

"Red Rot's called in the choppers," Boggs said. "The tunnel's close, though. If we hurry, we can still make it."

"Here we go again," R.J. moaned.

Blue put the truck into gear and rattled off along the rocky terrain. Mark noticed that the area was covered with large expanses of granite rock, which made the going easier.

Following Boggs' directions, Blue drove over the hill and into a narrow box canyon. The steep cliffs around them shielded them from view in most directions. The chopper sounded nearer, and suddenly its searchlights swept over the canyon's entrance behind them.

"The tunnel's just to the right of those trees," Boggs said. "Move it!"

Blue pulled the truck into thick foliage near a rocky overhang. The helicopters flew over and hovered momentarily. Three powerful lights scanned the ground near the truck, then continued west.

Mark let out a breath. "That was close."

Blue grabbed a flashlight from the glove box, and they all got out. Blue shined the light into the tunnel. It looked about thirty feet deep and was tall enough to stand up in. They went into the tunnel and waited for the chopper to disappear. Blue was still rubbing his wrist, but he seemed all right. "What happened back there?" he asked.

R.J. quickly explained the events at the gate.

"This Red Rot dude is crazy to think he can steal the space shuttle," Blue said. "We gotta hike outta here and call the Marines."

Boggs shook his head. "By now Red Rot has made General Robbins order a full perimeter shutdown. Security teams will be patrolling the fences with acoustic dishes, infrared scanners, and guard dogs."

"Guard dogs?" Blue said. "I wish Miss Fluffy was here—almost."

Miss Fluffy had lived in the back of the dog truck before Mark adopted her. She and Blue had a long-running feud—Miss Fluffy did the feuding and Blue did the running.

"How does Red Rot control the general?" R.J. asked.

"He injected him with a BioBot," Colonel Boggs said. "BioBots are the result of a highly classified government program."

"I know about the BioBots," R.J. said, "but they aren't used for mind control. They simply allow humans to control animals' actions."

"That's not exactly true," Boggs said. "I shouldn't say anything, but given what's happened, I'll bend the rules." He paused. "After your father invented the BioBots, the Air Force hired another company, Genetron Physics, to build a microscopic control module—the MasterBot."

Mark was lost. "What's that?" he asked.

"The MasterBot was supposed to control the BioBots mentally," Boggs continued. "One MasterBot is injected into the human controller who can then manipulate the actions of all BioBots. Theoretically, at least."

"What do you mean 'theoretically'?" R.J. asked. "Didn't the MasterBot work?"

"Unfortunately, no," Boggs said. "Genetron was never able to perfect the MasterBot's mental telemetry link. It was too complex for them. The best they did was invent a device called the BioVoice, which required a vocal input."

"That's what Red Rot had," Mark said, remembering the small microphone on the man's collar.

"Correct," Boggs answered. "He stole it along with the BioTels. That's when Professor Rowberry was rehired to perfect an external mental telemetry unit. It fits around the neck and sends mental commands directly to the BioBots. He called it the BioTel."

"My father should have been hired in the first place," R.J. said. "The Genetron engineers are nothing but hackers."

Mark still heard the drone of helicopters in the distance. "How did Red Rot get involved?" he asked.

Boggs thought for a moment. "That's a long story, but I'll try to make it short. Vandenberg Air Force Base launches military payloads into space—mainly communication and spy satellites. England, as America's closest ally, also uses Vandenberg to launch their military satellites. Red Rot was the security director for the English government, and the Nanny was his bodyguard. Red Rot got wind of the BioBot program and decided to steal some. He broke into the program area, stole the BioBots and a BioVoice, and conducted human experiments."

"Human experiments?" Blue asked.

"Correct," Boggs said. "And they worked just like they did on chimps—total mind control. It's not surprising, actually. More than 98 percent of chimpanzees' genetic material is identical to humans. It was only pure luck that I inspected the BioBot program area one night and found Red Rot and the Nanny sneaking out with a box of BioBots and a BioVoice. Britain convicted Red Rot and the Nanny of treason and sent them away for good—or so I thought. You know the rest."

Mark's mind was reeling. "So using the BioBots, Red Rot has a good chance of stealing the space shuttle?"

"A very good chance," Boggs said. "Especially since he seems to have brought his own team of space controllers laid-off from the Johnson Space Center."

"But who can Red Rot sell a space shuttle to?" Blue asked. "It would kinda stand out at the swap meet."

Boggs smiled. "Of course, once Red Rot steals the *Explorer*, it could never be taken into space again. That would be too obvious. But it could be taken apart by engineers from any unfriendly country. Then, using the *Explorer* as a blueprint, a relatively cheap copy could be built within a few years. An unfriendly country could become a world space power almost overnight. The *Explorer* is worth millions of dollars on the black market. Because it only requires a 5,000-foot runway to land, Red Rot could be taking it anywhere—he might already have a buyer."

"Probably Nimrod," Mark said.

Boggs perked up. "Nimrod?"

"Don't you remember?" Mark said. "Red Rot told us that Nimrod would have no use for us. That's why he tried to kill us."

Boggs nodded to himself. "Sounds like an inside contact. Nimrod is probably the code name of a high-placed military officer on base. He could be anyone."

"We certainly can't unmask Nimrod while we're stuck in this tunnel," R.J. said.

Boggs nodded. "It's too bad you gave away Congo and the BioTels at your house. The *Explorer* would be grounded without them. Luckily I wasn't captured, and without me to link with Congo and fly the shuttle, Red Rot and Nimrod can't take the *Explorer* anywhere."

"So that means Red Rot will be looking for you," Mark said.

Boggs nodded. "We've got to get out of here before he gets across the river."

"But how?" Blue asked. "You said the base was surrounded by an electric fence."

Boggs thought for a moment. "Correct. But they can't put an electric fence in water. Vandenberg sits on miles of Pacific Ocean coastline. If we had a raft, we could paddle down the coast to Lompoc and call for help."

"But where do we get a raft?" Mark asked.

"We'll make one," Boggs said. He looked at

Blue. "Do you have any inner tubes?"

"Only the ones in the tires."

"How about an air pump?" Boggs pressed.

Blue nodded. "Listen, I got enough tools in this clunker to float the Titanic."

"Excellent," Boggs said. "Let's get started."

"This will be perfect!" Mark said, feeling hopeful again. "What could go wrong?"

Boggs cleared his throat. "I suppose I shouldn't say anything, but . . ."

"But what?" Blue asked.

"The waters around here are infested with sharks—great white sharks."

H₂ Uh, Oh

The moon slowly rose into the eastern sky, casting a soft glow on the canyon. Working feverishly, Blue and Colonel Boggs jacked up the truck, braced the axles with rocks, then removed the wheels. Mark began deflating the tires, and Blue and Boggs pulled them free of the rims and extracted the tubes. R.J. held the flashlight and gave unneeded advice. Using the 12-volt compressor from the tool box, Blue began inflating the tubes.

While the inner tubes inflated, Mark took the flashlight and wandered into the tunnel. Toward the back, his toe hit something metallic. He bent down and found a three-foot diameter metal grate. Although the compressor was making a racket from the front of the tunnel, Mark thought he heard running water under the grate. He returned to the truck.

"What's the manhole cover in the tunnel

for?" Mark asked the colonel.

"It leads to an underground aqueduct," Boggs answered. "The Explorer's engines are extremely loud. The launch pad has to be blanketed with a pool of water during liftoff to keep the sound waves from bouncing up and damaging the shuttle. The water flows into a million-gallon holding tank on base. The pool is filled just before launch."

"So why is the water running now?" Mark asked.

Boggs' eyes widened, and he motioned for Blue to turn off the compressor. He listened for a moment. "This is bad," he said, hearing the water rush beneath from the tunnel. "The holding tank is already being filled. That means the launch schedule has been moved up. Nimrod must have great authority. We've got to hurry."

"Is there a way to get a message out quickly?" Mark asked. "Maybe we can stop him."

Boggs thought for a moment. "The water flows through tunnels that lead to the storage tank under the Command Bunker. If we could get to the storage tank, we could go up the inspection hatch leading into the bunker. From there, we could make our way to the satellite communications room and send a message to the Pentagon."

Mark thought it sounded risky. The water

seemed to be moving swiftly through the underground tunnel. "Do you think we should try it?" he asked.

Boggs shook his head. "Even if we survived the current, we would never find the Command Bunker. There are dozens of tunnels down there, all intersecting like a huge maze—and the only map to them is on the wall in the Security Center. Besides, even if we got into the bunker, we'd be walking right into Red Rot's hands. His men are swarming over the complex. We're better off trying the rafts."

They finished inflating the tubes, then followed Boggs through the trees to the base of a cliff. There, they found a rockfall that formed a natural staircase.

Colonel Boggs pointed up the cliff. "We'll climb up here, then head west to the ocean. Stay close to me and don't . . ."

The hillside lit up as a Humvee roared up the box canyon, its powerful searchlight sweeping the ground. "Freeze!" Red Rot's voice blared through a loudspeaker. "We followed your tire marks! You're surrounded!"

"That's impossible," R.J. said. "The canyon floor is solid rock."

The Humvee let loose a blast from its .50 caliber machine gun. The four sprinted into the cover of the trees as the powerful slugs tore off branches and rained chunks of rock on their heads.

"Stay here!" Boggs said. "I'll draw their fire!"

"But they'll kill you!" Mark objected.

"No, they need me," Boggs said. "But they don't need you. You're the ones in danger. I'll try to distract them. Get back to the tunnel and hide until they leave. Then go to the coast and bring help!"

Boggs darted away from the trees and into the canyon. Machine gun fire threw up a spray of dirt behind him. The Humvee's bright headlights silhouetted him as he wove back and forth across the canyon. As he neared it, the Nanny stepped out of the door and raised her knitting needle to her lips. Seconds later Boggs slapped his neck and stopped running. As if in a trance, he stood still, then walked slowly to the Humvee. Red Rot and two of his men grabbed Boggs and pulled him into the vehicle.

"They darted him," Mark said. "Back to the tunnel."

Mark heard a roaring sound in front of him, and an Apache helicopter gunship suddenly shot up the cliff face in front of them. It circled over the three boys, blasting them with a hurricane-force wind. Mark looked up and saw its rocket tubes aiming toward them.

"It's going to fire!" Mark yelled over the wind blast.

They ran into the tunnel as a salvo of Hellfire missiles detonated behind them, bathing the entrance in incandescent light and scorching heat. The three boys were thrown forward by the concussion, their clothes smoldering from the inferno. Outside, the trees were engulfed in flames, sucking masses of oxygen out of the tunnel.

"I can't breathe!" R.J. said, choking on the fumes. His eyelids fluttered, then his eyes rolled back in his head, and he fainted.

Mark's lungs burned from the heated air. He put his face to the ground to get under the smoke, and a cool breeze hit his cheeks. He opened his eyes and saw the grate he had found earlier. Running water echoed far below.

An amplified voice blasted into the tunnel. "Stay clear!" It was Red Rot's voice. "We're going to collapse the cave entrance!"

All shooting stopped, and the Humvee backed away. Moments later the only noise was the sound of the hovering helicopter. Mark realized the troops had moved out of the blast area to allow the helicopter to rocket the cave entrance. "Get the grate off!" Mark yelled, rising to his knees. "They're going to bury us!"

Blue scrambled forward, slid his fingers

through the grate and pulled. Nothing happened. "It's stuck!" he yelled. "Help!" Mark went to the other side, put his fingers in the slots and pulled with all his might. "It's moving," Blue said, straining. "Harder!"

Suddenly the grate came free, and both boys fell backwards.

"Go, Blue!" Mark yelled. "Down the shaft! I'll get R.J."

"No!" Blue yelled. "You'll never be able to move him by yourself."

Mark nodded and they grabbed R.J., lifted him over the grate, and dropped him. Water splashed as R.J. hit far below. Then Blue jumped down the hole, feet first.

Moments later, Mark dropped in after him. He scraped the rough concrete walls most of the way down, then the hole seemed to widen. He hit the water sideways, plunged to the bottom of the aqueduct then pushed up and broke the surface. Mark braced his feet against the rough bottom to resist the current. His side ached and his head pounded, but at least he was alive. As his eyes adjusted to the dark, Mark saw that the waterway was faintly lit by small bulbs set in the ceiling. A shadow came toward him. It was Blue with R.J. limply in tow.

"He's breathin'," Blue said, "but not much else." Mark saw an ugly welt on R.J.'s forehead and noticed that his half-opened eyes were glazed.

A low, violent rumble came from overhead. "Get away from the shaft!" Mark yelled. "There's going to be an avalanche! They've opened fire!"

Mark turned and stroked wildly with the current. Blue grabbed R.J. in a lifesaving hold and kicked powerfully, pulling even with Mark. Moments later, massive chunks of loose concrete crashed into the water around them.

"Dive!" Mark yelled. He saw Blue drag R.J. down as he went to the bottom of the channel. The water churned violently as shock waves rippled the aqueduct. Mark stayed down as long as he could then burst to the surface, gasping. The hot air smelled like gunpowder, but the concrete had stopped falling. Mark sucked in a huge breath.

Blue broke the surface beside him, dragging up R.J., who was coughing and sputtering. "I was gonna wait a little longer," Blue said, breathing normally, "but Fishberry didn't look so good."

R.J. coughed for several moments then took a few normal breaths. His face regained color and his eyes lost their glassy look. The cold water had brought him to his senses. He looked at Mark and Blue and nodded weakly. "I'm okay," he said.

Mark looked around. They were in an eight-foot diameter concrete and brick tunnel filled with about five feet of water. "Boggs said this is the underground water system that feeds the storage tank under the Command Bunker," Mark said.

"So how do we get out?" Blue asked.

R.J. shook his head. "Didn't you listen to Colonel Boggs? This aqueduct is a maze of tunnels, and we don't have a map. We're trapped down here forever!"

A Chimp Off the Old Block

After an hour swimming in and out of passageways, Mark knew they were lost. R.J. was complaining of fatigue, and Blue was complaining about R.J. They finally found a muddy platform above the waterline where they could rest. Mark and Blue pulled themselves out of the water then hoisted R.J. up, the big kid groaning and complaining.

"I don't know why you're having such a hard time, Floatberry," Blue said. "You should be harder to sink than the yellow rubber duck in Harrison's bathtub."

"It's red, not yellow," Mark said, defensively.

Blue and R.J. looked at each other then laughed, "I didn't think you actually had a rubber ducky, Harrison," Blue said. "I was kidding."

Mark felt his face turn red. He was glad the tunnel light was dim. "It belongs to Clint," he said, hoping they believed him.

"I wish I had a younger brother I could blame things on," R.J. said, flopping onto his back.

"It usually ends up being the other way around," Mark noted. "Clint blames me for everything."

"I think I got an older brother," Blue said. "I seen an old picture once of me and my sister at some big kid's birthday party. I asked Allie about it, but she wouldn't say nothin'."

Mark figured that talking was better than worrying—and certainly better than giving up. "What makes you think he was your brother?" he asked.

"He had me in a headlock," Blue said. "Only another Berzoni could do that to me. My face was really blue."

"Hey," Mark said. "Maybe that's where you got your name."

Blue thought for a moment. "Naw, that don't fit. My name ain't Headlock." He shifted around, unable to get comfortable. "I got a lump in my pocket." He reached into his back pocket and pulled out a plastic case. "My headphone case! I thought I lost it. I got no use for it, now, though. My boom box's all smashed up. Might as well toss this." He drew his arm back to throw the case.

R.J. eyes suddenly widened. "Wait! That isn't a headphone case. That's the BioTel case!"

He stared at Blue. "I thought you gave it to the men at my house!"

Blue seemed confused. "Me too. I musta' got the two cases mixed up when I dropped 'em in your room."

"So Blue gave the two men his headphones instead," Mark said. "Red Rot has Congo, but he doesn't have the BioTels. Maybe they can't launch the space shuttle after all?"

"Perhaps," R.J. said. "But when Red Rot discovers that he has Blue's headphones instead of the BioTels, he'll come after us. We've made ourselves even bigger targets. We have to get help."

"How are we gonna do that?" Blue asked. "We're in an underground tunnel with no way out."

"Not necessarily," Mark responded. He grabbed the case from Blue. "This could be our way out."

"How do you figure that?" R.J. asked. "We can't make a signaling device from it. The BioTels are worthless down here."

"Don't you remember?" Mark said. "Boggs said there's a map of the aqueduct system on the wall of the Security Center. If we could see that map, maybe we could find our way to the hatch under the Command Bunker."

"But we can't *see* the map," R.J. said. "All the

BioTels are good for is interfacing with animals who are injected with BioBots."

"That's my whole point," Mark said. "We can't see the map, but maybe Congo can."

R.J. turned and stared at Mark. "Of course! Red Rot took Congo into the Command Bunker. If you can get into Congo's body and find the map, we'd know how to get out of here. Mark, you're a genius."

Mark was surprised. Usually, R.J. only called himself a genius.

R.J.'s brows furrowed again. "But there is a problem. The BioTel will put a person into the closest BioBot, and there's bound to be many different animals in the Animal Research Laboratory injected with BioBots. If Mark gets into an animal other than Congo, he might not be mobile enough to find the map."

Mark nodded. "I see your point. A snake, for example, wouldn't be able to turn a doorknob."

"Correct," R.J. said. "There'd be a better chance of finding a suitable animal if we all went."

"I ain't sure about that," Blue said warily. "I don't wanna go inside any animal."

"We either do that or die from hypothermia and exposure in these tunnels," R.J. said. "We have no other hope of ever getting out."

"Well, when you put it that way," Blue said,

"what are we waitin' for?"

R.J. took three BioTels from the plastic case and opened each unit's electronics panel. "I'm setting up a software timer so the interface will automatically break after thirty minutes. Otherwise, with no one here to turn off the units, we might be trapped inside the animals forever." He passed the units out to everyone and then adjusted the BioTels' metal sensors to contact the back of each person's head. "Start units on my signal," R.J. said. "Now!"

Mark pressed the small switch on the side. His vision blurred, then his eyes gradually refocused. He was inside a metal cage in a large room. Rows of various-sized cages containing different animals surrounded him. Mark looked down at his hand, wondering which animal his BioTel had projected him into. Amazingly, he saw the furry hand of a chimpanzee. He had made it! He was inside Congo. He beat his chest and hooted excitedly. He stopped as he realized he sounded like a real chimp! That was his only way to express himself.

Mark gazed at the walls but saw no map. He was in the wrong room, as expected. Mark looked down the long row of cages, wondering which animals R.J. and Blue were in. But there was no way to tell. He had to find a way out first. Then he could search for them.

He surveyed his cage for something to help him out. It was bare except for a small water basin in a corner and a light bulb in the ceiling. Mark grabbed the ceiling bars, swung to the side and looked out. He couldn't believe his luck—a large metal key ring hung on the wall outside his cage. He reached through the bars, but the keys were barely out of reach. Frustrated, he tried again, stretching until his arm and shoulder burned with pain. No luck—he was still an inch away.

Mark dropped to the floor of the cage and thought. He had to get out of the cage so he could find the room the map was in. He looked up, searching for an answer. It was right in front of him.

Mark scrambled to the top bar again. He held the bar with his left hand then braced one of his feet on a bar below it. He was amazed at how strong he was. Then, holding onto the bars by one hand and one foot, he reached toward the middle of the ceiling. His fingers touched the light bulb. It was hot, but by turning it quickly and letting go several times, he was able to unscrew it. He held the bulb in his hands and blew on it, cooling it down. Then, gently, he hit it against the wall and broke the glass. The fragments showered down.

Pulling the last of the glass off the bulb, he held the metal threads in his fingers and slipped his hand through the bars. The two glass prongs that had been inside the bulb, holding the tungsten filament, now extended out of it two inches. Reaching as far as he could, he slipped one of the prongs through the key ring and lifted it off the hook. Carefully retracting his arm, he grabbed the keys with his other hand and clutched the keys to his chest. He raced down to the floor, reached through the bars, and unlocked his cage.

Mark hooted loudly with excitement. He was free.

A chorus of answering calls burst out. Barking dogs, chirping birds, bleating sheep, and other animals joined in a loud ruckus. Mark walked down the aisle on his knuckles, looking in every cage, trying to spot R.J. and Blue. A big German shepherd stuck his nose through the cage nearest the front door. Maybe that was Blue. Mark reached out to try the door.

The dog barked savagely, bared it's fangs, and threw itself against the bars. Mark leaped away and saw a sign on the cage's back wall: "Trained Attack Dog. Extreme Danger." Mark leaped away and moved down the aisle. The dog quieted.

Mark stopped in the middle of the row. Blue and R.J. had to be somewhere. "Where are you guys?" Mark called out. What sounded like speech in Mark's mind hit his ears as a series of chimp hoots.

"Harrison?" a voice said behind him. "That you?"

Mark spun around and looked into the ferocious stare of a peregrine falcon. Perched inside a cage, the falcon turned its head quizzically. "You in the monkey, Harrison?" Mark suddenly realized that his ears were hearing the sharp cawing of a falcon, but his mind was hearing the voice of Blue. They were talking mind to mind!

"You're a falcon, Blue," Mark said.

The falcon flapped its wings and fluttered around the cage before landing. "This feels weird, Harrison. But kinda cool, too."

"I told you it wasn't that bad," Mark said. "I didn't think we'd be able to talk to each other, though."

"Don't get any ideas," Blue cawed again. "You call me an airhead an' I'll play woodpecker on your nose. Now get me out of here. We gotta find that map."

Mark unlocked Blue's cage, and he burst from the cage like a shot. "I don't see Fatberry."

Low, grunting snorts came from the end of the room, and Mark heard a distinctive voice in his head. "Of course you can't see me, you dolt. I'm caged. The BioTel interface is allowing us to speak mentally. Now, get over here and free me."

Mark and Blue followed the low snorts toward the back of the room.

R.J. continued talking. "I can't see my feet, so I'm not sure what animal I'm in. It does feel like something large and dangerous, though. Be careful. I could be a giant Kodiak bear of the wild Canadian Klondike. Or perhaps a fearsome white rhinoceros from the untamed African plains."

Mark and Blue stopped in front of R.J.'s cage. Mark was dumfounded by what he saw, but Blue immediately let out a series of high choppy caws that registered in Mark's mind as uncontrolled laughter.

"Oh you're dangerous, all right," Blue chirped. "But only at the dinner table. Come to think of it, you ain't changed much at all."

Mark tried not to laugh. R.J. was inside a pot-bellied pig. "You're a porker, R.J."

"And you're a monkey's uncle," R.J. shot back. "But I still consider you my friend. Now, open the cage and tell me what I am."

Mark put the key in the lock and opened the door. "I wasn't calling you names," Mark hooted slowly. "You're inside a pig."

Blue burst into another series of high-pitched screeches.

"This is an outrage!" R.J. snorted. "This animal makes a mockery of my muscular physique. I am insulted."

"The pig's probably thinkin' the same thing," Blue said. "You always wanted to be a famous scientist. I always said you were a real ham." He suddenly stopped flying and lighted on R.J.'s broad back. "Somebody's comin' down the hallway!"

"Get off me," R.J. grunted. "I'll not haul around a wisecracking prairie chicken."

"I hear footsteps, too," Mark hooted. "Everyone into the cage!" He jumped inside next to Blue and R.J. and shut the cage just as the main door opened.

Red Rot, the Nanny, and Colonel Boggs entered the room. Red Rot held a plastic case.

"That's the case I gave to those two guys at your house, Oinkberry," Blue cawed.

Boggs stopped and stared down the aisle. "Why is Congo caged with a pig and a falcon?" Boggs asked the others.

"Leonard and Pope were supposed to isolate him," the Nanny said angrily.

"Never mind," Red Rot said. "He looks safe. All we're here to do is test the BioTel interface to Congo to make sure Boggs can fly the shuttle." He opened the case, grabbed something, and handed it to Boggs. "Here, put on the BioTel."

"Colonel Boggs is still under Red Rot's control," Mark said quietly.

Boggs examined the object. "Wait a minute. This isn't going to work unless you've got a tape deck. This isn't a BioTel, you fool—it's a pair of stereo headphones!" He handed them back.

Red Rot looked at the headphones for a moment, then his face twisted in anger. "The kids tricked those two boneheads!" He threw the headphones across the room.

"Hey," Blue screeched, "those were expensive!"

"Shut up!" the Nanny said to the falcon. She looked back at Boggs. "So the kids must still have the BioTels."

Boggs nodded. "That would be my guess."

"We're going to have to dig them out of the cave and search them," Red Rot said. "Boggs can't fly the shuttle without a BioTel." He turned to the Nanny. "Call for a bulldozer then get half the men and meet us outside at the Humvees. We haven't got any time to waste if we're going to make the polar-orbit launch window and rendezvous with Red Storm."

"I can't go with you to look for those kids," Boggs said.

Red Rot nodded. "Very well. Wait for us in General Robbins' office. Or should I say Nimrod's office."

"Call it what you want," Boggs said.

They spun around and hurried from the room.

"General Robbins is Nimrod!" Mark hooted. "No wonder Red Rot was able to take over Vandenberg so easy."

"The Nanny only pretended to dart the general when we first saw him," R.J. said. "That way, if anyone sees him do something questionable, he has an alibi. The general can say that the BioBot made him do it. Very clever."

"But I never heard him mention 'Red Storm' before" Blue cawed. "What's that?"

"I don't know," R.J. snorted. "But I do know what a polar orbit is. It's a path around the earth that passes over the north and south poles. It's not nearly as common as an equatorial orbit—an orbit over the equator. And Vandenberg is the only launch base in North America positioned for polar orbits. But if Red Rot is just stealing the shuttle, why would they need to go into a polar orbit? They can reach any point on earth from an equatorial orbit."

Mark was troubled, but he knew they couldn't waste any more time talking about it. They had to find the map to the tunnels. "Let's give them a few minutes to leave the Command Bunker," Mark said, "then we'll search for the Security Center. We've got to be careful not to draw attention to ourselves."

"How we gonna do that, Harrison?" Blue screeched. "It ain't everyday you see a monkey, a pig, and a falcon hangin' out together. This ain't a dumb Disney movie, ya know."

"I know that," Mark said. "We'll just have to

distract the guards. I've got a plan."

"It better be good," R.J. grunted. "We've got to find the map this trip. We can't afford to come back once the timers kick in. If Red Rot searches the aqueduct and finds our bodies while we're inside these animals, we'll be totally helpless!"

Animal House

"That's the last one," Mark hooted. "All the animals are out—except the attack dog."

Using the key, he had opened all the cages and released the test animals into the Command Bunker. Dogs, cats, mice, rats, pigeons, and several sheep rushed down the corridor. When Red Rot's men found them, it would create a diversion. "Get R.J.," he said to Blue, who was perched on top of the door.

Blue fluttered away to the back of the room, screeched sharply several times, then raced back. "Oinkberry won't come."

"Why not?" Mark asked. "We've got to hurry."

"He's eating dog food," Blue answered flatly. "He already ate all the other food, including my birdseed and the paper plate it was on."

"I'll get him," Mark said, swinging between his arms toward the dog cage.

"Better take an umbrella," Blue warned.

70

"The slobber's really flyin'."

Mark stopped in front of the cage R.J. was in. The pig had not only eaten all the food from the basin, but he had also broken into the automatic feeder and was crunching away at the last morsels. "Are you finished?" Mark hooted.

The pig snorted and looked at Mark. "I can't help myself. I never realized dog food could be so delicious." He dove back into the hard morsels.

"Get a grip, R.J.," Mark said. "The pig's feeding instincts are taking over. You must be getting a feedback loop from the BioTel."

"Can't talk," R.J. grunted between mouthfuls. "Must eat."

Blue fluttered next to Mark. "Don't forget, Harrison, Oinkberry likes your mom's horrible cookin'. Gravy Train has gotta be a treat compared to that."

"No argument, there," Mark said. "Blue, fly down the corridor and find the Security Center. Boggs said the aqueduct map was on the wall."

Blue stretched his wings. "Okay, but if I find the map, you gotta keep Oinkberry from eatin' it." He fluttered down the room and into the corridor just as R.J. finished chomping.

"Don't listen to Blue, R.J.," Mark hooted. "I know you won't eat the map."

"I wonder if the map paper is new or recycled?" R.J. snorted, licking his lips. "The bird food dish was a vintage corrugated cardboard. Quite tasty."

Mark decided he'd keep R.J. away from the map after all. He led the snorting porker out of the room and into the hallway.

"Attention, all personnel," Leonard's voice blared from a hallway loudspeaker. "The test animals have escaped from the Research Center. Apprehend and return them to their cages!"

Blue flashed toward them and landed on R.J.'s back. "I found the room. I'll give you directions." He fluttered from R.J.'s back to his head. "Hey, this is like an aircraft carrier, except bigger."

With R.J. leading the way, and Mark loping along behind, they followed Blue's directions. They made a left, then turned right into a long hallway. Pope was at the end of it, holding an assault rifle.

"There you are, Chimp," Pope said. "You and your two friends are goin' back to the slammer." He waved his arms and moved toward them.

"I'm gonna attack," Blue cawed. "The room's just around the corridor."

"You're too far away," Mark hooted. "He'll shoot you. I'll lure him closer." Mark leaped in front of R.J. and moved his arms, mimicking Pope.

"You know me, don't you, Congo?" Pope

said. "You remember all the bananas I gave you today. Remember how to do this?" Still walking, he raised his left arm in the air and scratched his head.

Mark copied him.

Pope laughed. "You're a smart one, aren't you?" He moved closer and scratched one armpit.

Mark mimicked Pope's motion. "A few more steps, Blue," Mark hooted. "Get ready."

Laughing aloud, Pope put the rifle down and walked forward on his knuckles, hooting like a monkey. "Try this, Congo."

With the gun on the floor, Mark saw his chance. "Now, Blue!"

Blue let out a spine-tingling screech and exploded forward, aiming at Pope's head with a blur of flashing wings.

Pope screamed and dove away in terror. He scrambled for his rifle with one hand and fended off Blue's clawing talons with the other.

"Hop on, Mark!" R.J. squealed. "I'll hit him low and you hit him high!"

Mark hopped on R.J.'s back and held onto the pig's ears. Grunting loudly, the enraged porker charged forward like a freight train. Mark bounced up and down on its back like a bronco rider.

Ahead, Pope lay on the floor swiping at the falcon. He grabbed his rifle and raised to one knee, drawing a bead. Loud grunts drew Pope's attention. "Not the pig!" He screamed and pulled the trigger at the same time.

R.J. and Mark plowed into Pope, slamming him back. R.J.'s snout plowed into his stomach, doubling him over. At the same time, Mark threw his arms up, raking the rifle upwards and sending the burst of bullets harmlessly into the ceiling.

"You got him!" Blue cawed triumphantly.

Pope rolled on the floor, gasping for breath. R.J. charged him again and hammered him against a wall.

"Shots fired!" Leonard's voice carried down faintly from a distant hallway. "Look in Section C!"

"Let's get out of here," Mark said. "We can't get caught in the corridor."

"We're almost there," Blue squawked. "One more hallway. Follow me." He fluttered into the air.

R.J. got off the gasping man and broke into a trot. Mark raced along behind, turned right, then sprinted to the last door on the left. A white sign spelled out Command Bunker Security Center.

"Open the door," Mark said, seeing his friends standing still.

"In case you forgot, Mark," R.J. grunted. "You're the only one with hands."

"Oh, yeah." Mark leaped on R.J.'s back and turned the knob with both hands. They rushed in, and Mark slammed the door behind them. Video monitors and reel-to-reel tape machines lined both sides of the room. At the far end, Mark saw a large map tacked to the wall.

They rushed forward and studied the jumbled maze of black map lines.

After only a minute, R.J. tilted his head toward the top corner of the map. "That three-way junction must be where our bodies are now. To reach the inspection hatch, we take three right-hand passages then go left at the last inter-section."

R.J. looked at the security monitors. Cameras in each hallway showed Red Rot's men running down the halls. "They're coming this way," R.J. said. "But we only have a few minutes until the timing circuits kick in and disconnect the BioTel links. We can wait here until we transfer back into our own bodies."

"No," Mark said. "If we're found here, they might shoot us. Well, you two at least. These animals don't deserve that. We've got to get them back to their cages."

"You're right," R.J. said. "I didn't think of that." He studied the monitors. "If we follow the last corridor and turn right at the final junction, we should be able to sneak by the search team."

"Let's go!" Mark said. "Blue, you scout ahead."

Blue shot away. Voices grew louder as Mark and R.J. scampered into the corridor. Moments later, Blue flew up from behind and landed on R.J.'s head.

"Look for a place to hide," Blue cawed. "Leonard and his men are just around the corner."

Mark saw a sign by a door. "In here!" The sign read: Satellite Communications Room. He opened the door and shut it behind them. Footsteps pounded down the corridor and stopped outside the door.

"They must have come this way," Pope said. "I'm telling you the truth, Leonard. That chimp was riding on the pig like a cowboy—and the falcon was obeying the chimp's commands."

"Don't lie because you let the animals escape," Leonard said harshly.

"We gotta double back," Pope insisted. "If the chimp gets the rest of the animals to join his rebel army, we won't stand a chance."

Leonard sighed wearily. "If you've been drinking again, Pope . . ."

"No, I'm serious!"

"All right, we'll try it your way a little longer." Their footsteps retreated and finally disappeared.

Mark looked around the room and saw that it was filled with switchboards, satellite receiving gear, and antenna positioning controls. "Boggs said we could get a message through to the Pentagon from here," he said.

"Of course," R.J. grunted. "I'll tell you how to run the equipment. We'll send for help right now."

"We're as good as saved," Blue said. "It's about time we got a break. Get callin'."

Mark leaped to the control console and, under R.J.'s direction, quickly threw a series of switches and turned several dials. A high-pitched frequency filled the air, and a voice came over the main speaker. "This is Lieutenant Colt at the Pentagon Communications Command Center. We have received your access signal, Vandenberg. Please respond with today's password."

"I don't know the password," Mark said excitedly. "This is an emergency! Vandenberg Air Base has been taken over by a group of hijackers led by Sir Redford Rottingham. Please send in the Marines. Red Rot plans to steal the space shuttle *Explorer.*"

There was a pause, then Colt answered. "You trying to fool me, Sam? Because that's the worst monkey imitation I've ever heard."

Mark slapped his head. He'd been speaking with Blue and R.J. so easily through the mental BioTel link that he'd forgotten he could only talk like a chimpanzee. To Lieutenant Colt, he sounded like a chattering idiot.

"No, wait!" R.J. burst in. "He's telling the truth. We need help!"

"Oh, a pig now, huh, Sam?" Colt answered. "Did Captain Chi tell you I was taking my kids to the zoo tomorrow? This some kind of practical joke"

Blue fluttered up to the microphone. "You're the only joke around here, dude. You better listen to us or I'm gonna . . ."

"That supposed to be a dodo bird, Sam?" Colt interrupted. "Nice try. But if you think I'm gonna report this and make myself look like an idiot, you're crazy. Don't call again unless you're willing to give the password. Pentagon out." The satellite link disconnected.

Mark shook his head in frustration. They had no chance of getting a message through. All Lieutenant Colt had heard was a monkey chattering, a pig snorting, and a bird screeching. Even if they could talk, they didn't have the password. Trying again was useless. "Let's get back to the cages," Mark said. "The BioTel link is going to break any minute."

He opened the door, and they raced off. They made two quick turns then hurried into the research center. Hearing voices coming around the corner, Mark rushed R.J. and Blue into their cages. He got back into his just as the front door opened. Leonard, Pope, and three other men in black camouflage combat suits walked in.

Pope's mouth gaped open as he saw the chimp, the pig, and the falcon sitting sedately in their cages. "No, it can't be. The chimp was a cowboy, and the pig was his horse, and . . ."

Leonard cuffed Pope on the head. "I warned you about drinking on duty. See what it's doing to you? It's making you see things."

"No," Pope pleaded. "I quit drinking years ago. This is all the chimp's fault."

"Strip search this man," Leonard ordered the three troopers. "And don't be gentle about it. I've got a feeling he's packing a bottle."

The BioTel started to disconnect, and Mark's vision blurred. The last thing Mark saw before he faded out of Congo's body was the three troopers grabbing Pope's arms and pulling his pants down around his ankles.

Eat and Retreat

Mark's blurred vision cleared, and the underground aqueduct appeared before him. Even though he was still underground, he was relieved to be back in his own body. Something tickled his lip, and he brought his hand up and wiped away a squishy object from his mouth. A half-eaten worm fell to the floor.

"Ahhh!" Mark screamed. He bent over and spit repeatedly. At his feet lay a small pile of wriggling worms—Congo had been feeding again. Mark jumped up and rushed to the aqueduct. Sticking his head over the edge of the platform, he gulped a mouthful of water and swished it inside his mouth.

"How did I get so filthy?" R.J. thundered from behind Mark.

Mark turned and saw R.J. lying belly-down in a mud pile. The pig that came into R.J.'s body had decided it needed a bath—a slime bath. R.J.

took his BioTel off and slid into the water by Mark. Dunking himself repeatedly, he scrubbed off the slippery muck. Mark put his and R.J.'s BioTels in the plastic case and slipped it into his back pocket.

"Where's Blue?" he asked.

R.J. shook the water from his eyes. "I don't know. He certainly didn't fly away."

"Don't be so sure, Mudberry," Blue's voice came from above. "How else did I get up here?"

Mark looked up and saw Blue perched on two protruding bricks several feet above the platform. Bits of straw and twigs formed a small circle underneath him. The falcon had built itself a nest.

"Have you laid any eggs yet?" R.J. called.

"One more crack outta you and I'm gonna fry some bacon." Blue said. He pushed off the bricks and landed beside them. He took his BioTel off his neck and stuffed it into his back pocket.

"Let's get moving," Mark suggested, feeling cold again. "I want to get inside."

"I agree," R.J. replied. "If we follow the right tributary, we should get to the . . ."

"The ventilation grate's off!" Red Rot's faint voice floated down the tunnel. "They've gone into the aqueduct. Bring the ropes!"

Mark looked at R.J. "We waded in a big circle! Red Rot's right behind us."

"The tunnel acoustics might be deceiving,"

R.J. said. "Red Rot could be a mile away and sound like he's next door." He thought for a moment. "Of course, the reverse might also be true."

"Time to do some more scout work," Blue said excitedly. "Be right back." He two running steps, flapped his arms vigorously, and leaped into the air. For a split second he arched upward gracefully, then he dropped like a rock and belly-flopped into R.J.'s mud pile. Blue lay still for a moment then pushed himself up, moaning. He was covered with mud. "I forgot I'm not a falcon, anymore." He dragged himself out of the mud and slipped into the water.

"Check all the tunnels within 500 feet," Red Rot's voice echoed again. "The Nanny and I are going back to the Command Bunker. Call me if you find something."

"Let's get going," Mark urged, slipping into the cold water next to his friends. "Blue, you take point—but follow R.J.'s directions."

"Yeah, sure," Blue grumbled. "Just don't expect me to fly any more scout missions."

Blue led them through the maze of tunnels as R.J. confidently called out directions at each junction. Mark was amazed at R.J.'s memory. As they moved farther down the waterway, the sounds of Red Rot's search became fainter, then disappeared.

The water deepened until Mark couldn't touch bottom. Soon they were at another junction, and had to paddle against the current to keep from being swept into the wrong canal. Blue seemed fine, but R.J.'s breathing became loud and ragged.

"Let's take a break," Mark said. He anchored himself on a protruding brick and grabbed R.J.'s shirt, stopping him in the stream. Blue stayed in the middle of the channel, treading water easily against the current's pull.

"How much farther?" Mark asked.

"We should almost be there," R.J. gasped. "The left tunnel at the next junction should lead to the storage tank. Just be sure and stay out of the far right passage. It's an overflow channel that drains into the ocean."

"Maybe we just oughta take that one," Blue suggested. "We still might be able to make it to Lompoc."

"No," R.J. said. "According to the map, it comes out on a sixty-foot cliff. We'd be smashed on the rocks below."

"It's the Command Bunker or nothing, then," Mark said. "Let's go."

R.J. drifted into the current with Mark close behind. Blue kicked hard and stroked out ahead. After only a few feet the stream sped up as the tunnel angled sharply downward. They slammed against the tunnel walls, bobbing helplessly like corks. The swift water began roaring.

"Stay together!" Mark yelled. He kicked up for a moment and saw that the channel ahead emptied into a strangely churning pool. At the pool's far end were two exit channels. The one to the left led to the storage tank, Mark realized, and the right one to the cliff. Spitting water, he swam as close as he could to the left wall.

"Stay left!" he yelled. All three were swept down into the pool.

A low rumbling, like the suction of a giant vacuum cleaner, echoed in the cavern. Mark stared toward the middle of the pool in horror— no wonder the water was churning. A huge whirlpool, twenty feet across, had been formed by water going down a bottom drain. The only way to the left passage was across the swirling pool.

"Stay on the outside!" Mark yelled. "Don't get sucked in!"

Blue stroked hard and skirted the outer edge of the swirling water, heading for the left tunnel.

R.J. suddenly swung toward the middle, and his head bobbed under. Moments later he popped up again, clawing frantically in the water. "The whirlpool's got me! Help!"

"Fight it!" Mark yelled. He reached out to R.J. but felt a sharp jerk as the whirlpool yanked on his legs.

"It's too strong!" R.J. yelled, feebly stroking against the irresistible force.

Blue, nearly to the left channel, heard the yells behind him. He turned, saw Mark and R.J. being sucked in, and stroked back, kicking up a white wake behind him.

"Help R.J.!" Mark yelled. "I can make it myself!"

Blue hesitated, looked into Mark's eyes, then nodded. He plunged into the whirlpool and grabbed R.J.'s collar. Blue tried to kick both of them free, but the current was too strong. The two circled the whirlpool, spinning closer to the deadly center.

Mark put his face into the water and stroked until his shoulders burned with fatigue. He paused and saw that he was closer to the center, not farther away. He couldn't break free. Letting himself spin around the whirlpool for a moment, he looked for his friends.

They were gone. Either Blue had broken free and gotten them out of the pool, or they had been sucked under.

The current tugged harder at Mark's legs. He made another frantic effort to kick free, but the water clutched him in an icy grip. Spinning in a tight circle, the vortex pulled him inward. Mark was surprised by its power and realized it was useless to struggle. He took one final breath and was sucked under.

Spinning madly, he went down twenty feet, his lungs burning in pain. His ears hurt, then suddenly popped. He hit something hard, but couldn't tell if it was a floor or a wall. He hit again and realized it was the concrete floor next to the drain hole. His air was gone.

An underwater current suddenly threw him sideways and slammed him against a far wall. The water out there was almost still. Fighting the nearly overwhelming instinct to inhale, he pushed against the floor and shot upward. Air rushed into his lungs as he reached the surface. Spitting water and gasping, he looked around, disoriented.

His heart sank. His friends were still gone, and he was too tired to fight anymore. He floated on his back and let the current pull him toward the whirlpool. Would the drain send him over the sixty-foot cliff, or into the storage tank? It didn't really matter. He'd be dead before he reached either one.

He thought of Blue and R.J. and hoped they were safe.

Then he was sucked under again and everything went black.

Nimrod

"Breathe, Harrison! Breathe!"

The words sounded distant and unreal to Mark. He felt like he was floating on a calm, warm lake and was about to fall asleep. He decided to ignore the voice and just drift off . . .

"Ahhh!" A bomb exploded in Mark's chest, wrenching a cry from his lips. Mark's eyes shot open and he saw Blue, to his side, raising his fist into the air. R.J. was directly above him, his mouth pressed hard against Mark's, exhaling deeply. Another bomb went off as Blue pounded Mark's chest again. R.J. jerked back as Mark coughed up a geyser of water. Mark's chest heaved as he sucked in great, ragged breaths of air.

"He's breathing, Blue!" R.J. said, "and his heart's beating! Stop the CPR!"

Another racking cough split Mark's chest, and he spit up another fountain of water. Mark lay still, fighting for air through his violent retching.

Gradually, the spasms decreased until he was breathing easily.

He was in a small, concrete room next to an open floor hatch. A solitary light bulb hung from the ceiling, and a row of metal lockers stretched along the far wall. R.J. and Blue, both dripping wet, were crouched on either side of him looking very concerned. Mark pushed himself slowly to one elbow. "How did we get here?"

Blue shrugged. "After I dragged Leadberry outta the whirlpool, I went back for you. No big deal."

"Blue's being unusually modest," R.J. said, wiping off his mouth. "After saving me, Blue saw you going toward the whirlpool drain, which, by the way, leads to the cliff. He swam across and towed you back then pulled us both to the access ladder in the storage tank. Then he carried us up here to the Command Bunker through the inspection hatch."

"All that with one hand tied behind my back," Blue said.

Mark smiled weakly. "I thought I was dead."

"Yeah, well, you were," Blue answered.

"I was . . . dead?" Mark gulped

"Very much so," R.J. said. "When we got here, we found that your heart had stopped and you weren't breathing. It took us nearly two minutes to bring you back with CPR."

"It woulda' been sooner," Blue said, "except it took awhile to find a coin."

"A coin?" Mark asked. "For what?"

"To flip for who had to give you mouth-to-mouth," Blue said, looking disgusted. "R.J. lost, so he had to do the lip work. I got to pound on your chest."

"My life hinged on one toss of a coin?" Mark said in disbelief.

"Course not, Harrison," Blue said. "We went two outta three."

"It was only fair," R.J. nodded. "After all those worms you ate, your breath was disgusting."

Mark sat up, angry. "Next time I die I'll make sure I have some mouthwash in my pocket."

R.J. and Blue nodded gravely at each other. "Good idea, Harrison," Blue said. "Could save your life."

Mark staggered up. They had a lot of work to do. "Let's look in the lockers and see if there's any dry clothes. I've got an idea."

"I hope it's better than your last one," Blue said.

They began opening lockers. A minute later they found one full of coveralls with the words "Shuttle Technician" written on their backs. Mark gladly stuffed his wet, ragged clothes in a locker and put on the dry coveralls. He stuffed a BioTel in his pocket and left the case in the locker. The

BioTel had come in handy before, and it might again.

"Now what, Harrison?" Blue said. "We sneakin' outta this Command Bunker, or what?"

"What good would that do?" R.J. asked. "We'd just be captured again. I say we make a try for the Communications Center and call the Pentagon again."

"My plan exactly," Mark said. "But first we need to find Colonel Boggs and get the satellite password. The Pentagon won't talk to us without it. Red Rot told Boggs to wait in General Robbins' office. We've got some time before Red Rot and the Nanny get back from the tunnel. If we pretended that Red Rot darted us and then told us to get the satellite password, we might be able to trick Boggs."

"It's possible," R.J. said. "then with the password we could call the Pentagon."

Blue nodded. "I passed General Robbins' office when I was flyin' around. With half the guards gone, I bet we could sneak there, easy."

"Okay, then," Mark said, "let's go."

Blue stuck his head out the door and saw that the corridor was clear. Motioning Mark and R.J. forward, Blue set off briskly down the long hallway to the right. They made several turns then heard voices ahead.

"Get ready to run," Mark whispered.

"Don't panic," Blue said. "Look away to hide your face and walk normal. I ain't the number-one class cutter at Davis High for nothin'."

Four of Red Rot's black-camouflaged commandos approached. As they got closer, Mark saw that Pope and Leonard were in front.

"Sorry about pullin' your pants down," Leonard said to Pope.

Pope shrugged. "Don't worry about it. I'm just glad I had on a clean pair of shorts. I guess all those talks my mom gave me about wearing clean underwear really paid off, huh?"

Leonard shook his head. "You're a strange one, Pope." The four men didn't even look over as the three boys passed.

"Just like skippin' math," Blue said, turning a corner and leaving the group behind. "Robbins' office is just ahead."

They stopped in front of a mahogany door bearing the general's name. Mark put his ear to the wood, heard nothing, and pushed it open.

"He isn't here," R.J. said, disappointed.

Mark saw that General Robbins' office was actually a suite of rooms. The front room contained a secretary's desk and a row of file cabinets. A hallway led to three other doors.

"Me and R.J.'ll check in back," Blue said.

As his two friends left, Mark looked around the office. Pictures of the stern, white-haired general hung on each wall. They all showed Robbins hunting big game animals in different parts of the world. A big envelope sat on the secretary's desk. Mark idly opened it and removed a thick folder. He gasped as he read the handwriting on front: "Operation Red Storm. Authorized by Nimrod."

"Come here!" Mark called out. "I found something."

"Hope you did better than us," Blue said. "Boggs ain't back there."

Mark showed the folder to his two friends. R.J. grabbed it and scanned it quickly. "This is terrible," R.J. said, quickly turning pages and speed reading. "But it all makes sense! How could I have been so blind?" He handed the folder back to Mark, his face white and hands trembling.

"What is it?" Mark asked tensely.

"There's no doubt about Nimrod at all, anymore," R.J. said. "He is General Robbins. Nimrod just isn't Red Rot's contact—he's in charge. And he isn't just trying to steal the space shuttle—it's much worse than that."

"How could anything be worse?" Blue asked.

R.J. pointed to the paper. "Robbins plans to use the space shuttle to reach an abandoned CIA missile platform called Red Storm."

Blue looked confused. "What's a missile platform?"

R.J. answered impatiently. "It's a military space station. It circles the earth in a 500-mile-high polar orbit. Robbins is going to use the space shuttle to steal Red Storm's six nuclear warheads. Then, according to this, he plans to sell them to the highest bidders—for at least twenty-five million dollars each!"

Mark looked at the pictures of Colonel Robbins on the wall. Everything clicked in his mind. "The code name 'Nimrod' fits General Robbins," he said. "In ancient mythology Nimrod was a hunter, just like the general."

R.J. nodded grimly. "According to these documents, the CIA launched Red Storm illegally. They kept it secret from the President of the United States, the Congress, and the American people. General Robbins worked for the CIA at that time and was in charge of Red Storm security, so he knew all about it. This was during the Cold War when the CIA thought war with the Soviet Union was inevitable. When peace was declared, the CIA couldn't very well ask Congress for money to dismantle a space station that didn't officially exist. Everyone connected with the Red Storm program would have been sent to prison. So the CIA burned all the files and pretended that Red Storm never happened."

"But not General Robbins, right?" Blue said.

R.J. nodded. "It appears that when he was

passed over for promotion to the Joint Chiefs of Staff, last year, he decided to have his revenge." He looked at the paper again and shook his head. "Red Rot had nothing to do with stealing the BioBots and the BioVoice. That's all a cover story. Robbins smuggled the devices into Parkhurst Prison himself, helped Red Rot and the Nanny escape, and then recruited former rocket controllers from Johnson Space Center to run the Command Center. It's all in here: names, dates, times, everything."

"But those nuclear weapons could fall into the hands of terrorists," Mark said. "Millions could die."

R.J. nodded. "General Robbins is a cold-blooded monster."

A jumble of voices sounded in the hallway and footsteps came toward the door.

"We didn't find the boys," Red Rot's voice carried into the room. "They're undoubtedly lost in the tunnels. But we did find what we were looking for." The doorknob slowly began turning.

Mark looked at Blue and R.J. in horror. General Robbins' office only had one door.

They were trapped inside with nowhere to run!

Circuit Breaker

Mark stuffed the folder into his shirt. "Quick," he whispered. "Into the back room!" The three rushed into the back room and shut the door. Racks of metal filing cabinets sat in long rows under a strong fluorescent light.

Mark saw a black phone on a desk. One of the buttons on it read: "Intercom Receive." "Maybe we can listen to them," Mark said. He pushed the button.

As the intercom engaged, Mark heard the main door to the outer office open. Several sets of footsteps entered the suite from the hallway.

"The boys are dead," Red Rot said.

There was a pause, then Colonel Boggs' voice came over the intercom. "Are you sure?" He didn't sound happy.

"Yes, our men just found a BioTel near a whirlpool. It appears the kids got sucked down the exit drain—the one that empties onto the cliffs."

Blue quickly checked his back pocket. It was empty. Mark realized that Blue had lost his BioTel while saving him.

"There's no way they could have survived," the Nanny said. "With the undertow in that surf, I doubt their bodies will ever be discovered."

"So all systems are go, now," Red Rot said. "The launch is set for an hour. Colonel Boggs, you'll be taking the *Explorer* into polar orbit, using Congo."

"But we still haven't tested it on Congo," Boggs argued. "It might not work."

It seemed that Colonel Boggs was resisting the BioBot in his brain, Mark thought. Perhaps there was hope.

"We'll test it now." Red Rot said. "Pope and Leonard are bringing the BioTel and Congo here immediately."

"You don't give up easily," Boggs said.

"Nimrod doesn't pay me to give up," Red Rot answered.

Mark clicked off the intercom. "General Robbins is paying Red Rot and the Nanny," he said quietly.

Blue looked disgusted. "So what if we do know General Robbins is payin' 'em? We still got no way of stoppin' 'em."

Mark thought for a moment. "If only there was some way to destroy the BioBots."

R.J. shook his head. "Short of brain surgery, there's no way to remove a BioBot. And their micro-batteries last for months."

Mark stared at R.J. "Don't you have *any* ideas?"

R.J. cleared his throat. "There is no way to destroy the BioBots—but there might be a way to turn them off. I must warn you though, it has never been attempted because of the severe danger."

Mark didn't know whether to feel hopeful or not. "Is it more dangerous than Nimrod getting nuclear weapons?"

"Yes," R.J. said somberly, "for the person who attempts it." He paused, seeming to weigh the danger of his plan. "Colonel Boggs had my father put a virtual feedback loop in each BioTel's computer chip. If the virtual loop was activated, a person's mind could, theoretically, be projected inside a BioTel. From there, the person could follow the BioTel's data paths to the BioBot and shut it down."

Mark tried to understand. "So, if you turned on the virtual feedback loop, and I went into Congo again, I'd feel like I was inside the BioTel's computer instead of in Congo?"

"Correct," R.J. said.

"And then I could turn off the BioBot," Mark stated.

"Once you followed the data paths to it, yes."

Mark was confused. "So where's the danger?"

R.J. lowered his voice further. "My father never perfected the virtual loop. I can send you into the BioTel, but I can't bring you out. If I turned off the BioTel while you were still in the virtual loop, your neural brain cells would receive an electrical overload, causing irreversible brain damage." R.J. tapped his forehead. "The only way out would be . . ."

"What?" Mark pressed.

"For you to turn off the BioTel from inside the virtual loop. If you returned to the same spot where you entered the BioTel, and shut off all the data paths, the power supply would automatically deactivate without a power surge, thus bringing you safely out. Then, theoretically, you would come back to your own body."

"Theoretically?" Mark asked.

R.J. nodded. "Nobody has actually tried it."

"But what if I couldn't find my way back to where I'd entered?" Mark asked. "What would happen then?"

"Your mind would be lost. You'd be trapped inside the BioBot in Congo's brain forever. Your body would become a vegetable for the rest of your life."

"Don't do it, Harrison," Blue said quickly. "You could end up bein' a Brussels sprout. I hate Brussels sprouts."

After pondering R.J.'s words, Mark didn't see that he had much choice. "Millions of people might die if we let General Robbins get those weapons," he said. He pushed his hand into his front pocket. "I brought a BioTel." He brought it out and showed R.J. "Go ahead and modify it. I'm going into Congo's brain and shut off his BioBot."

R.J. nodded silently and took the device. Popping its small electronics case open, R.J. threw several tiny switches and turned two miniature dials. "There," he said, closing the machine, "it's done. Activating the virtual loop was far easier than disconnecting the BioBot will be."

Mark put the unit around his neck and adjusted the metal sensor so it contacted the base of his skull. "Wish me luck," he said. Without waiting for an answer, he turned on the BioTel.

Mark hoped he'd live to see his friends again.

Reality Check

Mark's eyes lost focus for a moment, and when his vision cleared, he gasped.

He was in another world.

He stood on a tall, black obelisk, perhaps twenty feet square. A desert of fine, white sand stretched to every horizon. Rivers of light cut across the desert from beneath the black rectangle, racing in all directions. Each river of light glowed a different color. Above, Mark saw a starless, black sky. R.J. had said that the BioTel had a virtual reality debugging loop. That meant the electronic circuits were being represented in a way that Mark could understand. He gazed over the alien landscape and tried to remember everything he'd learned about computers.

Computer chips were made from silicon, which was nothing more than sand. Therefore, the desert must represent the chip material itself. Within the chip were different data buses, which were pathways the information from the central processing unit flowed through. So that meant the square he was on was the BioTel's central processing unit, or CPU, and the rivers running outward had to be the computer data paths going to the BioBots. Each flowing river must represent the current of an electrical signal.

Mark jumped off the obelisk to the sand. He reached down and dipped his hand into a blue river. A brief vision flashed in his mind. He was in a cage looking down at a grunting pig. He jerked his hand out. The blue river had to be the data bus that led to the falcon's BioBot. Mark quickly went around the entire black obelisk, dipping his hand into each flowing data stream. Brief impressions of different animals flashed into his mind. Strangely, though, three of the data streams were dark and gave off no impressions at all. Maybe the BioTel wasn't working correctly. He'd have to remember to mention that to R.J.

Finally, Mark dipped his hand into an orange river. A tingle went through his body, and he had the distinct impression of unhappiness at being caged. This mind had more intelligence than the others. Brief flashes of thought burst into his mind: bars, a long room, a hairy leg. It was Congo's cage! Mark withdrew his hand. Now, how to follow the data bus to the chimp's BioBot?

The current in the orange river flowed quickly. But, if he could float down the underground aqueduct, he should be able to float down the data bus. As he looked around, he saw there was no choice. He took a deep breath and jumped in.

He expected to be carried along with the current, but instead he felt a quick burst of speed and the impression of angling upward. The sand quickly disappeared beneath him, then the river slowed. He bumped against something. Mark looked at his feet and saw that the river had turned into a long corridor.

Mark got out of the river and walked down the corridor. He saw small doors on each side of the corridor. Each door had a window set in it. He walked to one of the doors and looked through the window.

A dense jungle spread before him. Vines, creepers, and ferns were draped across giant trees that hid the sun. He saw a small chimp sitting near a tiny stream. A larger chimp, a female, approached the small chimp and began picking at its head, grooming it. Mark pulled back into the corridor. What did it mean? He was supposed to be inside the BioBot in Congo's brain. Instead, it seemed he was in a movie theater. R.J. obviously hadn't known about this effect. Mark went to another window and looked inside.

He saw an open grassland. A dense jungle stood several hundred yards away. Another chimpanzee, larger, was searching for termites near a mound of dirt. This was Congo, Mark realized. Behind Congo, was the rest of the chimpanzee troop. Suddenly, from behind a hill, a Range Rover truck appeared. The chimps scattered and ran for the jungle. The Range Rover pulled even with Congo, and two men in back threw a net. It settled over him, and Mark could almost feel Congo's panic. They lifted Congo into the back of the truck and put him into a steel cage. Congo's fear almost came through the window, and Mark pulled back.

So that was it, Mark realized. The corridor he stood on was the BioBot interface, and each door led to one of Congo's memories. The farther he went down the corridor, the more recent the memories became. Mark sprinted down the hallway until he came to the last door.

He looked through the window and saw the bars of the Animal Research Lab. He saw the pig that R.J. had transferred into and the falcon that Blue had entered. But Mark no longer saw Congo. Because he was in the present, he was now seeing through the chimp's own eyes.

The door at the end of the room opened, and Pope and Leonard walked toward his cage. Mark quickly understood; they were here to take Congo to General Robbins' office. He had to shut off the BioBot!

He raced back down the corridor and examined the place where the orange river disappeared into the corridor. A small gate let the river flow under the corridor. Mark looked to his right and saw a brown river flowing outward, in the opposite direction. It also came out through an open gate. Mark knew that a computer was controlled by a series of logic gates which directed the data flow. Therefore, the orange river must be the input data bus from the BioTel, and the brown river must be the data return channel. Both led to Congo's mind, and both were controlled by logic gates.

He reached down and slammed shut the gate to the orange river then darted back into the corridor. He looked through the first window and saw that it was dark. He'd done it! He'd shut off the BioBot! Now he had to get back to the BioTel and into his own body. There was no telling how long the output data bus would continue to function with the BioBot deactivated.

Mark could see that the brown river was already flowing slower. He had to hurry or he'd be trapped! Mark leaped up and dove into it. Instead of the instantaneous transport he'd felt coming in, though, he stayed underneath the brown river for what seemed like minutes. The

BioTel was shutting down, Mark realized, and the internal clock, which controlled its processing speed, was slowing, making the data stream falter. He had to get out!

Mark finally surfaced from the brown river and saw the black obelisk before him. As he scrambled onto it, he saw that the other rivers were gone. The only light in his world came from the faint, brown data bus. He had to get out before the clock shut down. But how? R.J. had said to turn off all the inputs and outputs. Perhaps he had to shut off the brown logic gate too. He looked down and saw a gate where the brown river flowed into the obelisk. Mark prayed he was doing the right thing.

He reached down and swung the gate closed. Instantly the brown river faded out, and the virtual world ceased to exist. As the darkness settled around him, Mark realized he'd never get out. He'd made a mistake. He closed his eyes, opened his mouth and screamed.

Airtight Alibi

"Shut up, Harrison," Blue ordered. "You're screamin' louder than Fatberry does when I eat the last piece of pizza."

Mark's eyes popped open. He was back in General Robbins' office, and Blue's hand was over his mouth. Mark nodded at Blue, who uncovered his mouth. "I'm okay," Mark whispered. "Did they hear me?"

Blue shook his head. "I think these rooms are soundproof."

"What happened?" R.J. asked. "Why did you scream?"

"I thought I was trapped inside Congo's mind," Mark said. He took a breath. "I think I turned off Congo's BioBot."

"How'd you do that?" Blue asked. "You barely closed your eyes before you started screamin'."

Mark shook his head. "No, I was in the virtual loop for at least an hour."

"You were thinking at computer speed," R.J. said. "What seemed like an hour for you was only seconds for us. Remember, it didn't really happen."

"It sure seemed real," Mark said, taking off the BioTel. "I thought the BioTel was broken. Three of the data streams were dark and weren't transferring data."

R.J. popped the BioTel open and adjusted the electronic settings. "Hmm. The BioTel was set to a narrow band transceiver frequency. I've widened it, now. Those other frequencies were probably just standby channels anyway." He handed the BioTel back to Mark.

Mark jammed the unit into his back pocket. "Turn the intercom back on. Red Rot's men should have Congo to the General's office by now."

Blue pushed a button on the phone. "Red Rot's got no idea we're listenin' to him," Blue said with a laugh. "For bein' an intelligence agent, he ain't very smart."

Mark put his finger over his lips, trying to stop Blue from talking. The three of them froze and listened.

Nothing came over the intercom. Then the door to the back room crashed open, flooding the dim room with light and freezing the three boys in place.

"No one move!" Red Rot yelled, pointing a chromed automatic pistol at them. He looked at Blue. "Next time you try to eavesdrop, try pressing the correct button. The intercom can send voices as well as receive them."

Blue's face fell in disappointment. "I really did it this time."

R.J. was furious. "Blue, you incomparable dolt!"

"Don't compliment me, R.J.," Blue said glumly. "I don't deserve it."

The Nanny crowded in behind Red Rot, pointing another pistol. Her gray hair and frumpy sweater were still in perfect order. "You three boys turn up in the most unlikely places," she said. "Get out front!"

Under Red Rot's gun, the three trooped into the front room, stopping beside Colonel Boggs. Pope and Leonard were there, with Congo between them. Pope held the BioTel from the tunnel.

"Sorry, Colonel," Mark said. "We didn't do a very good job of rescuing you."

"Shut up!" Red Rot screamed.

"Red Rot is in control," Boggs said blankly.

Red Rot put his gun to Mark's head. "How much do you know?"

"Nothing," Mark said. "We were only trying to get out of the aqueduct and get warm. We found a hatch and it led up into this bunker."

"What's this then?" the Nanny asked, ripping Nimrod's folder from Mark's shirt.

Red Rot nodded. "So you know it all, huh?"

Mark had no choice but to bluff. He tried to sound as confident as possible. "We know that General Robbins is Nimrod, and we know you plan to steal nuclear weapons from Red Storm and sell them on the international arms market. We've already put in a call to the Pentagon from the Satellite Communications Center. In a few minutes Vandenberg will be flooded with commandos. You better surrender to us right now."

Red Rot looked at Boggs. "Is that possible, Colonel?"

"Don't say nothin'!" Blue burst out. "They'll . . ."

The Nanny stepped forward and jammed her pistol into Blue's face. "Shut up!"

Colonel Boggs shook his head. "I must answer. The boys don't know the satellite transmission code. They can't call out."

"So much for the commandos," Red Rot said. He looked at his watch. "The shuttle flies in less than an hour. Go ahead and test the BioTel on Congo."

Boggs nodded and took the device from Pope. He slipped it around his neck and turned it on. Mark saw Boggs' eyes glaze over as the

BioTel interfaced with his brain. If Congo started acting like a man, and Boggs like a chimp, Mark would know he'd failed to shut off Congo's BioBot. Boggs eyes refocused, and he looked around. He suddenly dropped to all fours and sniffed the air. Then he lifted up his back foot and scratched the side of his head. Smelling the ground, Boggs walked forward growling, and stuck his nose in Pope's pants.

"Stop that," Pope said, jumping back. "I barely know you."

"What's going on?" Red Rot asked.

"I don't know," the Nanny said. "Boggs is acting very strange."

Of course, Mark thought. With Congo's BioBot turned off, Boggs had transferred into the animal containing the nearest BioBot—the German shepherd attack dog in the Animal Research Center. And the German shepherd was now in Boggs' body. With everybody's attention focused on Boggs, Mark slid next to Blue and R.J. "Get ready to run," he whispered.

Boggs turned toward the Nanny, his mouth open and tongue hanging out.

"Sic 'em, boy!" Mark yelled suddenly. "Attack!"

Boggs' lips turned up in a savage snarl as the trained beast within him reacted to the commands. Boggs barked ferociously, slobber dripping from his open mouth. He stalked toward the Nanny.

"He's gone mad!" the Nanny said, backing away.

"Pope! Leonard!" Red Rot shouted. "Get Boggs!"

As the two men moved forward, Mark shouted again. "Kill, Boy! Kill!"

Boggs gathered his feet beneath him and leaped for the Nanny's throat. Pope and Leonard jumped forward to intercept him just as he barreled into the Nanny. The tangled group, shouting, screaming and snarling, toppled together onto Red Rot, knocking him over. Congo jumped onto the desk, his wild hooting only adding to the confusion.

"Run for it!" Mark yelled.

Mark, Blue, and R.J. burst through the door and dashed down the hallway. The savage battle behind filled the corridor with screams of terror.

"Where to?" R.J. asked. "Boggs will snap out of it once the BioTel gets knocked off. We don't have much time."

"Let's go back to the inspection hatch in the storage room," Mark panted. "We can hide there and then escape back into the tunnels."

The boys twisted and turned through the maze of corridors until they came to the supply room. Darting inside, they slammed the door behind them and sank to the floor, panting for breath. Mark saw the inspection hatch on the floor, leading to the underground storage tank.

"We don't need to go back into the aqueduct," R.J. said. "When the shuttle doesn't launch on schedule tonight, the Air Force will send an investigation team here."

The loudspeaker in the ceiling blared into life. "Attention, all personnel," Red Rot's amplified voice boomed out. "Prepare the *Explorer* for manned launch. Colonel Boggs will be piloting the shuttle in person with myself and Misses Minnifield as crew members. The launch will go as planned in exactly fifty minutes."

A sick feeling crept into Mark's stomach as Red Rot's voice faded out. "We haven't stopped them at all," he said. "They're going to fly the *Explorer* themselves, hoping that Boggs can pilot it under BioVoice control. Nimrod's plan is still on schedule."

R.J. nodded. "It's a risk, but Boggs is a trained shuttle pilot. There's a good chance it will work."

"Can't you go inside Boggs' BioBot and turn it off, like you did to Congo's?" Blue asked.

"I thought about that," Mark said. "But when I was inside the BioTel before, I checked all the BioBot data streams but didn't find Boggs'. It's as if he wasn't there."

"It's possible Boggs is being shielded," R.J.

said. "Red Rot knows all about the BioBot program."

"We'd have to wreck the space shuttle to stop Red Rot, now," Mark said glumly.

"Actually, stopping the shuttle wouldn't be all that difficult," R.J. answered. "If we could get into the *Explorer's* cockpit, I could easily damage the controls. But we'd never make it past Red Rot's men."

Mark thought for a moment. "That's not true. I may know how to get to the shuttle."

"How, Harrison?" Blue said. "Fly?"

"No, swim," Mark answered. The idea had just formed in his mind. "Remember? Boggs said the storage tank under this room drains onto the launch pad to absorb the sound waves from the rocket engines. If we went down the hatch and were in the storage tank when the drain valves opened, we'd be splashed into the pool beneath the shuttle. Red Rot's men would never see us. We could just climb out and take the gantry elevator up to the cockpit. With these uniforms on, nobody would say a thing."

R.J. shook his head and moaned. "The thing I really hate about your harebrained schemes, Mark, is that they always have a chance of working. I can't say it's impossible."

"Count me in," Blue shrugged. "You just better hope Fatberry doesn't plug up the drain."

"Let's find some plastic sacks to put some more uniforms in," Mark said. "We can't sneak into the shuttle soaking wet."

The three quickly found a plastic sack in a locker and sealed three more suits in. Mark transferred his BioTel to one of the technician suits.

"Now let's get down the inspection hatch," Mark said, "and wait for . . ."

The room suddenly shuddered and, without warning, the corridor door locked solidly, and the inspection hatch snapped shut. Even the ventilation grates in the ceiling sealed off with loud clangs.

"Attention," the loudspeaker blared again. "The Command Bunker has been sealed off in preparation for the launch. All personnel are to remain at their stations."

Mark ran to the hatch and pulled on it, but it wouldn't budge. "It's locked!"

"The same goes for the door," Blue yelled out, yanking on the handle. "We're stuck!"

"If we can't get out!" Mark wailed. "We can't stop the shuttle!"

R.J. looked at the room and mumbled some figures under his breath. Finally, he looked at Blue and Mark, and his voice trembled. "That's not the worst of our troubles. The room's been hermetically sealed—it's airtight."

Blue sniffed the air. "You better not have gas."

"It's more serious than that, Blue," Mark said.

"Correct," R.J. said grimly. "This room only has enough air for the three of us to survive for twenty minutes, and the shuttle doesn't launch for fifty. We're all going to suffocate."

Royal Flush

"Hold your breath!" Blue urged. "The air will last longer." He sucked in a huge gulp.

"Don't be ridiculous, Blue," R.J. said. "Lack of oxygen can cause brain damage. Although in your case it would be impossible to notice."

"Recheck the lockers," Mark said, "and look for something to pry open the hatch with. We've got to get into the storage tank below."

Blue exhaled then kicked a metal trash can in frustration, sending the garbage flying. "We already looked through the lockers. There's nothin' we can use to escape. We'd need a stick of dynamite to blow open that hatch." He rummaged through the scattered trash. "And there ain't no dynamite here. There's nothin' but some empty soda cans, an old file, a rusty pipe, an empty Ajax can, and a matchbook." He slumped against the wall, struggling for breath.

"Carbon dioxide is already building up in the

room," R.J. said. "We might not even last twenty minutes."

Mark noticed the air getting stale, but they couldn't give up. As long as they could move, they had to try. "We've gotten out of worse jams than this before, R.J."

R.J. sat against the wall. "There's no way out, Mark."

"Are you sure?" Mark asked. "I thought science could solve any problem."

R.J. shut his eyes. "Something Blue said did give me an idea, but it's too dangerous."

"What's more dangerous than dyin'?" Blue said. "Tell me my idea."

"No, it won't work," R.J. repeated. "There's not enough oxygen."

"Not enough oxygen for what?" Mark persisted. "This might be our only hope."

"Very well," R.J. sighed. "But if it doesn't work, don't blame me. Aluminum powder and iron oxide are the main ingredients of a hot burning chemical compound called thermite. If we can file enough shavings from the cans and the pipe, *and* if there's enough oxygen, we can burn the hinges off the hatch. Thermite can melt any known steel."

"What?" Mark asked, perplexed. "You mean rust and aluminum can burn?"

"Yes, if they are mixed correctly to form

thermite. In fact, thermite burns at nearly the same temperature as the surface of the sun."

"Let's do it!" Blue said.

R.J. sighed. "Very well. We will try. But I'll need enough rust from the pipe and aluminum shavings to fill half the cleanser container."

Mark braced the pipe on the ground, and Blue filed vigorously. R.J. pulled the matches from the book and tied them together with string. Blue finished filing the pipe, then Mark held the soda can while Blue filed it down.

R.J. carefully tore the Ajax container in half. "The two powders have to be mixed exactly in a three to two proportion," he warned, "otherwise the thermite won't burn."

Mark struggled to breathe. The air was getting worse. R.J. scooped up the materials and poured them into the container. He put his hand over the top, shook it, and then placed it atop the hinge. R.J. then jammed the match bundle inside the container.

"Hurry, R.J.," Blue urged. "That ain't a milk shake. I'm gettin' lightheaded."

Mark too was gasping for breath.

R.J. hesitated. "If this doesn't work, we'll use up the last of the oxygen. We won't be able to breathe."

"We'll be dead anyway," Mark said.

"Yeah," Blue agreed. "What's another five

minutes? Let's get this over one way or another."

"Very well," R.J. said. "Get behind something. If it works, it will ignite any clothing within ten feet." He struck a match and lit the makeshift fuse. "Back away!"

They all crowded against the far wall as the matches burned down. Mark shut his eyes, praying the thermite would work.

A blinding light shot through Mark's eyelids. He spun around to face the wall as the thermite's intense heat blasted him from across the room. He had never seen anything so bright before—and his eyes were shut! The thermite hissed and popped, and thick smoke filled the room. The noise stopped and Mark opened his eyes. The intense brightness of the thermite was already fading but the heavy smoke made it almost impossible to breathe.

"Get the hatch open, Blue!" Mark yelled, his lungs burning with smoke.

Blue stumbled forward, grabbed the round handle, and jumped back. "It's hot!"

Mark went forward with the pipe and stuck it through the spokes on the hatch. Using the pipe as a lever, he pushed sideways. "Help, Blue!" he called out. Blue grabbed the pipe and gave it a shove. The hatch flew off, clattering against the wall. Fresh air rushed into the room.

"It's open!" Blue shouted. "Everybody down the ladder!"

R.J. hurried through the smoke-filled room to the hatch and climbed down. Mark and Blue were close behind. As Mark climbed down, he saw that the tank was about twenty feet across and thirty feet long. Underwater lights about ten feet down illuminated the bottom. Water poured in from a large pipe at one end of the tank. Mark guessed that was the passage Blue brought them through earlier.

"I got the plastic sack with the uniforms," Blue said from above. "Now what?"

A warning buzzer sounded in the corner of the room, and heavy machinery vibrated beneath them. A five-foot-diameter metal plate on the bottom of the pool slid open. The water level in the pool began dropping.

"The tank's draining onto the launch pad!" Mark yelled. "Jump!"

"I can't do it," R.J. said, holding onto the metal ladder. "It's too risky. I almost drowned before."

Blue climbed down next to R.J. "But we can't stop the *Explorer* without you," he said. "We don't know what controls to wreck."

"Forget it!" R.J. yelled back in panic. "I thought I could do it, but I can't. Enough is enough. No more water for me!"

"Leave him alone," Mark said quietly. "If we want to stop Red Rot and free Colonel Boggs, we'll have to do it ourselves."

Blue looked angry but nodded grudgingly. "Okay, Harrison, me and you. Go on three. One, two . . ." Blue reached over and pried R.J.'s hands off the rungs, ". . . three!"

R.J.'s eyes widened in surprise as he plummeted into the water. Moments later he was caught by the twisting whirlpool forming above the drain. "It's got me!" R.J. screamed. He took a gulp of air then was spun violently around several times and sucked under.

"Flushed like a goldfish in a toilet bowl!" Blue yelled. "I better go next. If Fatberry plugs the drain, I gotta be there to unstop it. I just wish I had a toilet plunger." He breathed deeply, threw in the plastic bag and plunged in after it. The spinning vortex grabbed his legs and flung him around before taking him under.

Anxiety rose in Mark as he saw Blue sucked under. This whirlpool looked even more powerful than the one in the aqueduct. But he couldn't back out now. Shutting off his fear, he closed his eyes and jumped feet-first into the spinning water. The current grabbed his feet, almost taking off his shoes. Then it clutched his legs, and everything became a blur as his body rotated violently. A moment later he was pulled under. He hit the floor then was sucked down the drain.

As Mark shot down he slammed against the

sides of the narrow pipe. Spinning incredibly fast, he almost lost consciousness, then the pipe angled upward. His lungs began to burn, but he forced himself to hold his breath. He had to find air. The pipe leveled out, and he shot into the open and skipped across smooth water like a flat stone.

As he stopped skipping, his legs touched bottom. He tilted his head back and took a deep breath. Above him loomed three huge cones, looking like three great, inverted moon craters. Mark instantly recognized them as the space shuttle's giant rocket engine nozzles. Lights glittered all around the launch pad. Mark saw that the water was held in a concrete pond. He whirled around to look for his friends. They were across the pool, clinging to the side. The plastic sack with the dry technician suits bobbed next to Blue.

Mark stroked over to them.

"Pretty extreme, huh?" Blue said. "Better than Thunder Mountain at Disneyland."

"How can you think of fun at a time like this?" R.J. sputtered. "I'm not supposed to be here. You threw me in!"

"I had to," Blue shrugged. "Me and Harrison woulda' missed ya."

R.J. considered the comment. "I must admit you two *are* helpless without me."

"Let's get out of the water and change," Mark said.

Pulling themselves over the concrete apron, they hid behind a steel girder and changed into the dry clothes. The pad was relatively empty, and only a few scattered figures near the gantry were visible.

"Attention!" a loudspeaker blared. "Clear the launch pad! All personnel must evacuate to the Command Bunker immediately!"

Plumes of condensation from the fuel tanks drifted into Mark's view as the fuel lines were automatically reeled in. The shuttle would be launching in minutes. They had to quickly get inside the *Explorer's* cockpit and wreck the flight controls. Mark just hoped they could make it. If they failed to get in, they'd be barbecued like cheap steaks on the Fourth of July!

Stowaways to the Stars

They rushed to the gantry elevator. One of Red Rot's armed guards stood at the elevator entrance.

"Now what?" Blue hissed.

"We're dressed like technicians," R.J. said. "I'll bluff our way in. Do what I do."

"Eat a lot and use big words?" Blue asked.

"Quiet," Mark ordered, seeing the guard was almost within earshot.

R.J. walked up to the guard with Mark and Blue behind. "We need to run a fourth-level diagnostic on the magnetic tape degausser," R.J. said to the guard.

"Yeah," Blue said. "Not to mention a rebuild of the prizmaton farpwinkle."

The guard's eyes wrinkled in suspicion. "I never heard of that before."

R.J. elbowed Blue in the ribs. "Forgive my associate, he's rather new."

"I'm not worried about what he said," the

guard said. "A prizmaton farpwinkle sounds scientific enough to me." The man looked R.J. up and down. "I think you're tryin' to pull something over on me, though, tubby. I never heard of a magnetic degausser."

R.J.'s face turned crimson in anger. "It is a scientific device, you incredible . . ."

Blue slapped his hand over R.J.'s mouth. "He ain't used to bein' around someone as smart as me, so he gets mad easy."

"Yeah, well, he better be glad you're along to tell him what to do," the guard said, stepping aside. "Good luck with that farpwinkle."

The boys crowded into the elevator.

"I'll check the zandiddle vomitrax while I'm at it," Blue said as the door slid shut.

Blue took his hand off R.J.'s mouth, and R.J. prepared to cut loose with a volley of verbal abuse.

"Save it, R.J.," Mark said. "We're in, and that's all that matters . . . right?"

R.J. looked at Blue with narrowed eyes. "I'd like to put a zandiddle vomitrax down Blue's pants."

The wire-caged elevator rose quickly, and with each moment they got a better view of Vandenberg. At the top, an open catwalk led from the elevator to the *Explorer's* cockpit.

"Be careful," Mark said. "That's ten stories

straight down." Grasping the handrail tightly, he led the way inside.

The control deck was cramped with five contoured chairs spread in front of the large cockpit window. Instruments, dials, switches and displays took up nearly every inch of the cabin walls.

Blue looked around in wonder. "Where do we start?"

"With the farpwinkle perhaps?" R.J. said.

"Stop it, R.J.," Mark said. "We only have a few minutes."

"Sorry," R.J. answered. "You're quite right." He pointed to an instrument panel on the ceiling. "I believe that is the inertial guidance gyroscope control. If we were to open the panel . . ."

"Hold it," Blue said suddenly. "The elevator's comin' up again!"

Mark rushed to the door. Coming up the open-sided gantry elevator were three familiar figures. "Its Red Rot, the Nanny, and Colonel Boggs," Mark warned.

"No way!" Blue said. "I thought we had more time."

R.J. looked at the floor and saw a small window beneath them. An inset handle was near it. "The cargo compartment! Get in! It's our only choice."

They went to the round hatch in the floor.

Once the *Explorer* reached orbit, this floor would become the rear wall of the cabin. Blue yanked on the handle and opened the hatch just as the elevator arrived at the top of the gantry.

"Fast!" Mark urged.

Blue lowered R.J. in then pushed Mark down. Mark threw his arms up to cushion the fall. Moments later, Blue lowered himself in and shut the door firmly above them.

Footsteps sounded in the crews' compartment above them, and Red Rot's muffled voice carried into the cargo area. "Everything looks jolly good," he said.

"Strap in," Boggs said. "It's going to be a rough ride."

"The launch pad is clear!" Pope's voice suddenly blared over an internal loudspeaker. "All unauthorized personnel have left the area. The *Explorer* will launch in five minutes!"

Mark looked at R.J. and saw the same shocked expression he knew was on his own face.

"What now?" Blue asked.

The sound of metal rang against the side of the vehicle as the main hatch was sealed.

"We're locked in!" R.J. said. "There's no way out."

Soft illumination from a row of lights on the walls allowed Mark to look around. Lockers ringed the forty-foot cargo area, and nylon straps for securing cargo were mounted along the floor. There were no chairs to sit in, Mark realized.

"Tie yourselves down with the cargo straps," R.J. said, throwing himself down and intertwining his body in the netting. "Lie flat and keep your head against something soft."

"Can I use your stomach?" Blue said, dropping to the floor and copying R.J.

Mark wriggled into the interweaving cords and put himself as flat on the floor as he could.

"Ignite primary engines," Pope ordered.

The craft shuddered with immense power, and a deafening roar began to build up beneath them as the liquid oxygen and hydrogen engines begin to burn.

"Beginning the countdown!" Pope blared.

Mark tensed as Pope counted down over the loudspeaker. When he reached zero, Mark closed his eyes and crossed his fingers.

"Ignition!" Pope announced.

With the roar of a thousand giant waterfalls, the spacecraft's engines throttled up to full power. Sledgehammer acceleration hit Mark's chest, making him gasp and knocking the air out of his lungs. His body grew heavier and heavier from the tremendous thrust, and within seconds he found it nearly impossible to breathe. He tried to look over at R.J. and Blue, but his sight began to darken and his head pounded. He fought for air, but his chest muscles weren't strong enough to fight the titanic G-forces. A wet liquid sprayed across his face, and he realized his nose was spurting blood. He thought he heard R.J. scream and then Blue, but the engine noise made it impossible to tell. Spots appeared before his eyes and the far wall began to fade out. *So this is what it feels like to die,* he thought. Seconds later, he passed out.

Free Fall

Mark opened his eyes. A blurred face hovered directly over him. At first, he thought it was an angel, but angels didn't have stringy hair, beady eyes, and breath like a Saint Bernard's. His head began spinning, and Mark shut his eyes to avoid getting sick.

"Hey, Harrison, you alive?" the voice asked.

The voice didn't sound like an angel's, but Mark still wasn't sure. His thoughts were foggy, and his whole body ached. "I feel like an elephant stepped on me."

"Naw," the voice above him said, "I had my eye on Fatberry the whole time, and he ain't gone nowhere near you."

Mark's head cleared and he wiped his face. He knew it wasn't an angel for sure—it was Blue. Mark opened his eyes. He wasn't in heaven, either. He was aboard a stolen spaceship, heading away from Earth.

"I'll remember that comment, Blue," R.J. said, freeing himself from the cargo straps.

"That proves my point, Harrison," Blue said. "Elephants never forget." He pushed softly against the wall and floated across the cargo bay.

Mark tried to sit up but was still restrained by the straps he had wrapped around himself—which had probably saved his life. Freeing himself, he looked around. Blue was ten feet away, hovering in space. Of course! They were weightless! Blue pushed off the back wall and floated to Mark.

"Cool, huh?" Blue said. Stretching out, he touched the ceiling and did three quick somersaults in the air. He kicked his feet out, caught the wall with his toes, and stopped himself with a dull clang of shoes against metal.

"Silence, you dolt," R.J. whispered from behind, his voice carrying across the chamber. "You want Red Rot to hear us? He could open the cargo doors and expose us to the vacuum of space—which is very similar to the emptiness between your ears."

Mark saw that R.J. was floating in the back part of the cargo bay, searching through a row of lockers.

"You'd think Fatberry would be in a better mood," Blue said. "He ain't weighed this little since before he was a baby."

"I agree with R.J.," Mark said. "Keep it down."

"Fatberry's lookin' for food," Blue whispered. "We been up here twenty minutes now. He must be starvin'."

"I'm looking for spacesuits," R.J. stated. "Although if I find earplugs, I will gladly insert them to protect myself from your idiotic babbling."

"Help him, Blue," Mark said. "I'm going to see what Red Rot's up to."

"I'll make sure R.J. don't eat the spacesuits," Blue said. He pushed off the ceiling and drifted away.

Staying away from the cargo window, Mark pushed off the floor and floated forward. It was hard to believe he was actually in space. Everything had happened so fast that it seemed unreal. It was almost as if he were watching himself in a movie, rather than actually being there. One thing was painfully real, though—Red Rot.

Mark stopped against the forward bulkhead and peered cautiously through the window. Red Rot sat in the co-pilot's chair with his back to Mark. In front of him, the Asian continent filled the main window. Brown land masses and blue oceans slowly drifted beneath white tufts of clouds. Over the horizon of the earth, stars shone brilliantly—far brighter and piercing than anything Mark had seen before. For a moment he was transfixed by the incredible view, then Red Rot shifted to the left a little, and Mark's wonder was replaced with dread.

An immense silver object grew larger in the window. It looked like a giant, weight-lifting dumbbell, consisting of two large cylinders connected by a long tube. Mark knew that this was the secret CIA space station, Red Storm.

Pope's voice crackled over the radio link inside. "Vandenberg to *Explorer*. What is your status?"

Boggs came into view from the side and punched a button on the console. "The computerized controls are working perfectly," he reported. "Approach sequence has begun. We are preparing to dock with Red Storm."

The dumbbell-shaped station grew larger in the window until Mark could see that each of its two modules was larger than the *Explorer*. Just before the two spacecrafts collided, Mark heard maneuvering jets fire on the hull, and the *Explorer* slowed, moved sideways, then drifted toward a port on the station's left module. Red Storm now filled the entire screen. With a soft jolt, the orbiter mated with the station. Mechanical latches between the shuttle and space station interlocked, then snapped shut with a metallic clang. The *Explorer* had reached her destination, five hundred miles above the Earth's surface.

Something brushed his elbow. Mark looked back and saw R.J. and Blue crowding forward to see through the window also. At the back of the cargo bay, Mark saw three silvery man-shaped objects floating in the air.

"I found the space suits," R.J. said.

Inside the cockpit, Red Rot opened a side compartment and pulled out some silver space suits himself. The Englishman glanced back at the cargo bay window and the three boys jerked their heads out of sight. Flattened against the wall, Mark hoped that Red Rot hadn't seen them.

The radio crackled to life and Red Rot spoke. "*Explorer* to Vandenberg. We're preparing to board Red Storm and unload the nuclear weapons into the escape pod. We'll leave one nuclear device on board Red Storm and detonate it after we're clear. That will vaporize both the station and the *Explorer,* and destroy all evidence. When the station blows, evacuate the assault team from Vandenberg."

"Message received," Pope said. "We're tracking you on radar so we'll know when you're clear."

"So that's their plan," Mark whispered. "They never intended to return to earth aboard the shuttle at all. They're going to use Red

Storm's escape pod to steal the nuclear weapons and get back to earth."

R.J. was deep in thought. "Very clever," he finally said. "When the military learns that Red Storm and the *Explorer* exploded, they'll assume that the escape pod was destroyed with it. Red Rot will return undetected to earth. General Robbins will be able to sell the nuclear warheads at his leisure."

"We've got to get out of the cargo bay," Mark said. "If we're in here when they set off the nuclear device, it's bye-bye birdie."

"You mean fry-fry birdie," Blue said.

"Quiet," R.J. whispered. "They're leaving."

Red Rot shut the radio down. Turning away from the console, he quickly suited up. Then the Nanny and Boggs did the same. Red Rot floated to the front airlock and pulled a red lever. There was a hiss as the air pressure between Red Storm and the *Explorer* equalized. Then Red Rot opened the airlock door and floated through. Boggs and the Nanny followed.

Mark grabbed the hatch handle and tried to open it, but it refused to budge. "It's locked from the other side."

"From its appearance, it's probably an automatic exterior safety lock," R.J. said. "It engaged just before the launch. Now, short of using a cutting torch, there's no way to open it from this side."

"Great," Blue said. "We came here to save the world and end up like sardines in a can."

Mark thought for a moment, looking back at the huge cargo bay doors below him. "Maybe not. R.J., can you short-circuit the cargo doors and open them from in here?"

R.J. thought for a moment. "There's no sign of a safety lock, like the one on the cabin door. I suppose it's possible."

"But we'll die in space," Blue said.

Mark pointed at the space suits still floating against the back wall. "Not if we're wearing those."

"You mean go for a spacewalk, Harrison?" Blue said. "You nuts?"

"I tend to agree with Blue," R.J. said. "Our inexperience could be fatal."

"We're going to blow up anyway if we stay here," Mark said. "If we can use the escape pod ourselves, Red Rot will be stranded. The cavalry is not going to come riding down on horses, rescue us at the last moment, and stop Red Rot." Mark took a deep breath. "We *are* the cavalry."

"I feel like I just stepped into a pile of horse manure," Blue said. "But you talked me into it."

R.J. nodded. "You're right. I'd rather go down fighting. I just hope the escape pod has an autopilot."

Mark clapped them on the shoulders. "All right, then. Let's get to work on the door."

Following R.J.'s orders, Mark and Blue began tearing panels off every surface, exposing what seemed like miles and miles of wire. Blue rummaged through the lockers until be found a small emergency tool kit. R.J. examined the servo motors and locking mechanisms that controlled the huge cargo doors. After studying them for nearly twenty minutes, he declared that he had found the solution. Giving Mark and Blue each a pair of wire cutters, R.J. had them cut a series of color-coded wires leading into the main junction. R.J. then traced a power lead, cut it, and carefully stripped off the insulation.

"That should do it," R.J. said. "When the red and green wires touch, the door will open."

"All right," Mark said. "Let's get the space suits on."

"You sure this is gonna work, Harrison?" Blue said.

Mark nodded with a confidence he didn't feel. It was a desperate plan, but it was their only option. If they couldn't escape in the pod, they'd be marooned five hundred miles above the earth—waiting for a nuclear blast to scatter their atoms halfway across the galaxy.

Space Cowboys

"One, two, three, pull!" Blue grunted. "One, two, three, pull!"

Mark waved his gloved hand and stopped for a moment to catch his breath. He was in a space suit but hadn't put his helmet on yet. He and Blue were trying to get R.J. into a space suit—but it was a losing battle.

Blue threw up his hands in frustration. "Come on, R.J., you gotta try harder." R.J. was halfway into his suit. But it had gotten stuck under his bulging stomach.

"This suit was obviously intended for BioBot animal flights," R.J. huffed. "It was not meant for a man, but for a chimpanzee—and a skinny one at that."

"Tell ya' what, Bonzo," Blue said. "Suck in the gut and I'll give you a banana."

Mark was worried. Red Rot and his crew had entered Red Storm thirty minutes ago. They had to be well on their way to unloading all the missiles.

"Stand back, Harrison," Blue said. He floated above R.J., braced his feet on R.J.'s shoulders, and grabbed the stubborn spacesuit. "It's sausage time!"

"Get down from there!" R.J. cried. "I am quite capable of . . . Ahhh!"

With a mighty heave of his shoulders, Blue pulled up on the spacesuit. R.J.'s eyes widened as his stomach stretched up around his chest. His midsection actually looked thin for a moment, Mark thought. Then, with a final yank, the suit slid over the stomach and came to a stop under R.J.'s armpits. Blue let go and floated away, sweat streaming off his face.

"It is quite fortunate that my knowledge of Tibetan breathing techniques allowed me to modify my muscle distribution," R.J. said, pulling the suit on all the way.

"Don't yaks come from Tibet?" Blue asked, grabbing his helmet and latching it on. "Cause all you do is yak, yak, yak."

As Mark secured his helmet, R.J. popped his on and moved to the two exposed wires.

"Grab onto a handhold," R.J. said. "Anyone that floats away from the space station will be lost forever. We'll have to climb into the station, sneak into the escape pod, and try to fly it home."

Mark grabbed a piece of loose cargo netting. He wrapped one end around his waist and tied the other end to a metal brace on the wall.

"Here goes," R.J. said. He joined the two wires. There was a small spark between them, then the cargo door slid smoothly to the side.

Restrained by the webbing, Mark felt the air pull past him as it rushed into the vacuum of space. The buffeting ceased quickly, however, and he gazed down on the spectacular panorama of the Earth. The glimmering blue of the Pacific Ocean now was in striking contrast to the earth-tone colors of the American continents. Floating near the cargo door's lip, Mark could see from the peninsula of Baja California to the jewel-like Florida Keys. The earth looked like a magnificent cathedral.

Blue held onto Mark's tether and looked out the door. "This is just like my geography class," Blue said over his helmet radio. "Look down there. That's India."

R.J. peeked over Blue's shoulder. "No, Blue. That's South America."

"Oh, yeah," Blue said. He turned and pointed to the right. "Well, then, check out Hawaii. Aloha, baby!"

"Uh, sorry, Blue," Mark said, examining the expanse below. "That's Cuba."

"Blue's right," R.J. said. "This *is* like his

geography class—he never gets an answer right there, either."

Mark shifted his gaze from the earth to Red Storm. He pointed at a round, raised port at the end of the station. "R.J., do you think that's the missile launch tube?"

R.J. studied it for a moment then nodded. "It appears to be. Why?"

"If we could open the tube door," Mark said, "we might be able to go through it into the space station."

R.J. nodded. "That certainly makes sense."

"One problem," Blue said. "How do we get there across deep space?"

"We'll have to climb hand-over-hand along the outside of the station," R.J. said.

"No," Mark objected, "that will take too long. We'll have to push off and glide over."

"No way, Harrison!" Blue said. "If we miss, the next stop's Mars, or Pluto, or maybe even Goofy. There's gotta be a better way."

"There's no time to argue," Mark said. He untied the webbing from the brace and wrapped the loose end around his waist. "Follow me." Aiming as carefully as he could, he pushed off.

"You win, Harrison," Blue radioed. "Nobody lives forever—especially nobody who hangs out with you." Blue pushed off. Moments later R.J. followed.

Mark glided through the airless void. Away from the earth he saw thousands of brilliant stars. The Milky Way seemed close enough to touch. He glanced back. Blue, traveling about the same speed, was right behind him. R.J., though, hadn't pushed off as hard and was farther behind.

R.J.'s voice was suddenly filled with tension. "Mark, you're off course. You're going to miss the station."

Mark looked at the end of Red Storm. R.J. was right. He was going to miss the station by a good ten feet—and he had no way of stopping.

"We're both headed for space!" Blue yelled, panicking. "I shoulda known better than to follow you!"

Mark forced himself to think coolly. "No, Blue we'll be okay. I've got a plan."

"That's what got us in trouble in the first place!" Blue cried in panic.

"Just listen," Mark said. "I'm going to throw you one end of the cargo strap."

"That won't help," R.J. said, the tension still in his voice. "You didn't attach the other end to the shuttle." He paused, his voice becoming quieter. "You're not going to make it."

"We *are* going to make it!" Mark insisted. "This will work." He waved his arm at Blue. "Get ready to catch—now!" Mark pushed the coil toward Blue who reached out and grabbed it.

The missile tube was beside Mark now, sliding off to his left. Mark had to make his move now. "Pull toward me!"

Blue quickly pulled them together. "That didn't gain us nothin'," Blue said, "except now maybe I can slug ya."

"Tie the strap's free end around your waist," Mark said. "I'll push off you to get to the station. Then I'll reel you in."

"Of course!" R.J.'s voice came over the headset. "A reaction mass! One of Newton's Laws of Motion: For every action there is an equal and opposite reaction—it just might work!"

Mark put his feet against Blue's chest and aimed his back at the space station. He pushed hard, sending Blue spinning away, but propelling himself toward the missile tube. Red Storm grew larger and larger, but he was still slightly off course!

"Stretch, Mark!" R.J. yelled.

Mark neared the corner of Red Storm and reached as far as he could. His fingers brushed the silver metal, making his body pivot toward the ship. He tilted just enough to grab a support wire on the station's surface. He slammed against the station, but managed to hold on.

"Amazing, Harrison," Blue said. "You finally did somethin' right. Reel me in!"

Mark quickly gathered the straps and pulled Blue in. R.J. landed on Red Storm with room to spare and slid over to them.

"That was a close one, Mark," R.J. said. "We must be more careful in the future."

"I agree," Blue said. "Now let's get into the missile tube."

Mark took a deep breath. R.J. was right. That had been close. Too close.

Silently they clambered hand-over-hand to the tube. Blue hooked his fingers under the three-foot-round metal cover and yanked up, but it didn't budge. "Think we should try the doorbell?"

R.J. examined a metal panel next to the missile port. "Now that your muscles have failed, allow me to use my intellect." R.J. pressed the center of the small panel, and it popped open, revealing a tangle of wire, several circuit boards, and a small servo motor. R.J. nodded. "Very advanced—but well within my capabilities." R.J. pulled two wire leads from their metal sockets and switched them. Then he touched a wire from a circuit board to a metal socket on the motor. The hatch swung open. "The tube should lead into the missile room."

"Good work, R.J.," Mark said. "I'll go first." He floated down and glided in head first. When he reached the end of the dark, ten-foot long cylinder, he found another servo motor that looked like it controlled the inner hatch's lock. He put both hands on it and pushed. Although it was normally controlled by computer, Mark was able to push the metal clasp aside. A sudden blast of air gushed by him as the room vented air through the slight opening he had made.

He held on, and the current of air subsided. Pushing the hatch all the way open, he poked his head through the opening. Seeing that the launch room was empty, he floated in.

The metallic-walled room was perhaps twenty feet wide and forty feet long. Hydraulic tubes and electrical conduits snaked along the seven-foot ceiling. Six sinister-looking, blunt-nosed missiles, ten feet long and three feet in diameter, were mounted along a huge cylinder next to the missile tube. Mark moved closer to the missiles and saw the reason they looked so blunt: five of the nose cones had been removed. Strands of wire dangled to the floor next to broken circuit boards. Red Rot had obviously been in a hurry.

As Mark studied the missiles, he thought he heard a hiss of air. He spun around and saw R.J. and Blue floating near a control box on the wall. They had entered the station, closed the tube door and pressurized the missile room. R.J. watched a pressure gauge rise, then took off his helmet. Mark and Blue did likewise.

R.J. took a deep breath, then spoke. "That device you are studying is a Common Strategic Rotary Launcher. It's used on all air force strategic bombers. When the signal comes to fire, the Rotary Launcher will spin each missile into position over the tube and launch them like a six-shooter." R.J. examined the nose of a missile. "Oh, no! Five of the warheads have already been removed."

Blue floated next to R.J. "I got a bad feeling about this."

"Not as bad as it's going to be," a man said from across the room.

Mark whirled around. It was Red Rot and the Nanny.

"I don't know how you three got up here," Red Rot said. "But it'll be the last place you ever go."

"Where's Colonel Boggs?" Mark asked. "If you've hurt him, I'll . . ."

"You'll do what?" Red Rot said. "Tell your mommy on me? Your precious colonel is in the Tactical Command Center. He's perfectly safe—for the time being."

Blue studied them carefully for a moment. "You ain't got a gun, do ya?" He pushed off the wall and floated toward them. "Let's see how tough you are now."

"I wasn't going to shoot you," Red Rot said.

He turned to the Nanny. "Dart them."

"Look out, Blue!" Mark warned.

Blue tried to dodge, but the Nanny brought up her thin tube and puffed sharply. Blue slapped his neck. "That didn't hurt. I'm gonna . . ." his words drifted away.

"That rather calmed him," Red Rot said.

Mark dodged behind the launcher as the Nanny reloaded in a flash and puffed again.

R.J. bellowed and pawed at his neck as the dart hit home. "You can't do this to me," R.J. said. "My father invented the Bio . . ."

"I've finally shut you up," Red Rot said.

R.J. remained quiet.

Mark crouched behind the launcher. There was no place to run. By the time he managed to get the missile tube open, the Nanny would have plenty of time to dart him. He was trapped!

"It's five against one now," Red Rot said. "You might as well give up. Neither you nor your friends are going to make it back home. You've stuck your nose into my business for the last time. Now I'm going to chop it off."

Mything in Action

Mark ran his hands through the spacesuit's pockets looking for a weapon, but found nothing. He quickly peeled down the spacesuit top and searched the pockets of his orange coveralls. He felt something in his back pocket and pulled it out.

The BioTel. Of course! He had put it there after changing clothes.

"I suggest we surround him, Mrs. Minnifield," Red Rot said. "You approach him from the left, and I'll come at him on the right. You two boys guard the door. I daresay he won't escape this time."

An idea came to Mark. R.J. hadn't touched the BioTel since Mark had disabled Congo's BioBot. That meant that the BioTel's virtual feedback loop was still active—allowing him access to the BioBots circuitry. He remembered how slowly time had passed inside the virtual world.

Maybe he could go into the circuitry again and disable Blue's and R.J.'s BioBots before Red Rot got to him. Perhaps he could disable Colonel Boggs' BioBot as well.

Red Rot appeared twenty feet to Mark's left, then the Nanny floated around the far end of the launcher to his right.

"Good day, lad," she said. "Or should I say good night?" She began loading another BioBot dart in her knitting needle.

Mark jammed the BioTel over his head and slapped its sensor against the base of his neck. Just as the Nanny brought the blow gun to her lips, Mark turned the unit on. His vision blurred, and then he was in the BioTel's alien world.

He stood on the black, CPU obelisk again, surrounded by the white, silicon desert. The starless sky hovered above him. Ten rivers of light spoked out from under the obelisk—the input and output channels of five BioBots. The three darkened data streams he has seen before were now brightly-colored and functioning. When R.J. had increased the frequency range, the BioTel had gained access to them. Maybe they had just been standby channels as R.J. had said. Mark looked and saw that logic gates still controlled each river of light.

He had to act fast. Running across the obelisk he shut the logic gates on two data steams. He then spun around and headed across the obelisk for the three remaining streams.

A chilling thought stopped Mark. There were *five* active BioBot data streams here. There only should be *three:* Blue's, R.J.'s and Colonel Boggs'.

Where did the other two come from?

A crackling stream of electricity raced down from above, boring into the center of the obelisk. Surprised, Mark jumped aside, trying to protect himself. The stream of electricity continued to grow until it separated into two solid beams of light: a green input stream and a red output steam. A cold knot of tension gripped Mark's stomach.

Someone had found him. He had to hurry.

Racing to the three remaining data streams, Mark only had time enough to slam down the output logic gate of each one. Whoever those BioBots belonged to, would now be unable to receive any output command signals from the BioBot controller.

An immense figure, at least nine feet high, stepped onto the obelisk from the input stream. A black cloak swirled around its body, and a long hood covered its face and head. It pointed at Mark with a white, bony hand.

"You!" it rumbled in a deep voice. "You turned off my BioBots!"

Mark felt as if he were standing before the very face of death.

"You've gotten in my way for the last time," the figure proclaimed. It threw back it's hood. A skeleton's head stared at Mark. The eye sockets seemed to bore right though him, and Mark began to tremble in fear.

"I am Nimrod," it said, pointing at Mark, "and you are dead!" Nimrod looked at his skeletal hand, as if seeing himself for the first time. "What am I?" He seemed confused by his appearance.

Mark's thoughts raced. General Robbins must have found the BioTel case Mark had left in the Command Bunker. By monitoring the BioBot telemetry from earth, Robbins must have discovered that somebody was turning off the BioBots. Knowing this, the general had obviously modified one of the BioTels to go into the computer world. The computer's virtual feedback loop must be representing the general's appearance according to his own mental self-image. Because the general's mind was filled with hate and revenge, the computer had turned him into the very image of evil—Nimrod, the Hunter.

"Take a good look, General Robbins!" Mark called out. "Inside the computer, you are what you think you are—a monster!"

"General Robbins?" The skeletal figure

laughed. "You are quite mistaken. I am Nimrod! And you, my interfering friend, are finished. It appears that I can be anything I want to be in this world. I am limited only by my mind—and I have a very nasty imagination. You couldn't leave well enough alone, could you? You kept ruining my plans. Well, it ends here." He raised his arm, and a fireball covered his fist. "Flame thrower anyone?" A pillar of fire arched out from his hand, racing for Mark.

Mark dove to the side as the flaming bolt passed by him. The heat singed his clothes and blistered his skin. That felt real! Suddenly his pants burst into flame, and Mark rolled across the obelisk. *He needed a bucket of water!* Before the thought even left his mind, a bucket of water appeared in his hand. He doused the flames.

He had only thought of water and it had appeared.

"How about a little Greek mythology?" Nimrod asked. His skeleton face grew eyeballs and skin, and his body began to twist and turn in impossible ways. As Mark watched in a horrified trance, Nimrod's head changed into an eagle's head. Then his body transformed into a lion with wings. Nimrod had turned himself into a griffin—an imaginary creature of evil, half lion and half eagle. The griffin roared, beat it's wings and launched itself into the air. It circled above Mark then folded its wings and dove.

He had to tame the griffin! Instantly, a long bullwhip appeared in his right hand and a wooden chair in his left. A white pith helmet sat on his head. His pant legs were flared out at the thighs, with their cuffs tucked into knee-high black boots. Mark was suddenly embarrassed. He looked like Jungle Jim—a corny, jungle-movie character from the Late, Late Show. *Couldn't he think of anything better?* He barely had time to raise the chair before the griffin struck. The whip was jerked from his hand, and the chair was shattered into a thousand pieces. But Mark was unhurt and scrambled away.

The griffin circled upward, preparing for another attack. Mark ran to the other side of the obelisk and saw the red output stream traveling up into the sky. If he could get into it, it might take him away from the griffin. Then again, it might take him into another computer world—one more horrible than this one.

He heard the bloodcurdling scream of the attacking griffin, and decided he had no choice.

Just as the griffin's razor-sharp claws reached him, he jumped.

Memory Lane

Mark felt a quick burst of speed as he angled upward. The CPU quickly disappeared beneath him, then the light stream slowed. He bumped against something. Mark looked at his feet and saw that the river had turned into a long corridor. He had made it into the data stream before the griffin reached him, and now he was bumping against the BioBot corridor connected to Nimrod's brain.

Mark realized that he was in Nimrod's mind. If this was like the BioBot in Congo's brain, he'd find a series of doors set in a straight hallway. Instead, Mark saw that the main corridor looked more like a dark and twisting cavern. A cold wind blew, moaning like death. Mark shuddered. Where the pathways in Congo's mind had been straight and orderly, these pathways were dark and deformed. General Robbins must be insane for his mind to be so twisted and evil.

"Running away won't help you!" Nimrod yelled from outside the cavern entrance. "You can't hide inside my own brain!"

Nimrod had followed him through the data stream!

Mark ran deeper into the cavern, found a twisting passageway, and quickly grew confused as he ran through a maze of turns. Mark hoped he could lose Nimrod in the tunnels, then circle back, find the data stream, and travel back into his own body. For the time being, though, Nimrod was gone. Mark saw light coming from a window in a door. He ran to it and looked in.

A military parade ground was filled with young men in uniforms, each cadet standing at attention. Spectators filled a grandstand facing them. A large banner in front of the grandstand read: United States Air Force Academy Graduation. Before the grandstand stood a podium with a microphone. A tall man in a decorated general's uniform stepped up to the microphone, and applause erupted from the crowd.

The man raised his hand to quiet the crowd. "I'd now like you to hear a few words from this year's top graduating cadet: Pepper Boggs."

A youthful Colonel Boggs stepped to the microphone and waited for the crowd to quiet. Mark felt the intense pride of the young man at that moment. But why was General Robbins remembering this? Did he know Boggs at the Air Force Academy?

"I'm getting closer!" Nimrod bellowed.

Mark turned but didn't see him. He dashed from the door and sprinted down another twisting corridor. He looked back but still didn't see Nimrod. Mark stopped and listened. Had Nimrod made himself invisible? Anything was possible. Mark began running again.

Mark went to another lighted window and stopped. He peered into the window and saw Colonel Boggs again, older now. He was in a cockpit of a jet fighter screaming over a dense jungle—it had to be Vietnam. Boggs was flying a bombing mission over enemy territory.

But something didn't feel right. Mark pulled back from the window and thought. Why would General Robbins have so many memories of Colonel Boggs—especially as a young man? In fact, *how* could he have a memory of Boggs alone in a jet? How would Robbins even know about it, unless . . . ?

Mark ran down the passageway looking for another window. He had to find the answer. He pressed his face against another window.

Boggs again.

The colonel looked his current age now. He stood in front of three generals sitting at an oval table. They were flanked by American flags. A small sign by a door read: "Joint Chiefs of Staff—Pentagon."

One of the generals spoke. "I understand your disappointment, Colonel Boggs, at not being chosen to command Vandenberg Air Base. We've decided to give that position to General Robbins."

Colonel Boggs' face twisted in rage. Mark felt waves of hate flow from him. "You can't do this! I'm more qualified. I'm a certified space shuttle pilot!"

"So is General Robbins, and he has more experience," the general said.

"But you promised me!" Boggs raged.

"Get a hold of yourself, Colonel!" the general said. "You'll take our orders and like them! If not, you'll be drummed out of the service entirely."

Boggs quieted and nodded tersely. But Mark felt the hate intensify. Hate—mixed with revenge. Boggs was going to make the Air Force pay for this humiliation, no matter what it took.

Mark turned away from the scene, sick with emotion. He had been wrong all along. General Robbins wasn't Nimrod. Colonel Boggs was! And Boggs was here on Red Storm! The man he had thought was his friend was actually an insane criminal.

Mark ran down the corridor and looked in several more windows. He saw Boggs stealing a MasterBot from a vault and injecting it into himself. He saw Boggs changing the MasterBot test results to show that they had failed. Mark saw Boggs secretly setting fire to the rest of the MasterBots.

So the MasterBot invented by Genetron *had* worked! Boggs had deceived everyone into thinking the device was a failure so he would have the only one.

Mark looked in another window and saw Boggs walking up to Red Rot and the Nanny in the Animal Test Lab. Boggs raised a blow gun to his lips and darted them both.

Mark's mind reeled as he turned away from the window. Boggs had darted Red Rot and the Nanny! He had been in control of them the entire time, manipulating them with silent commands through the MasterBot mental telemetry link. The two English agents had been set up and sent to prison by Boggs. They were victims too!

And Mark had once considered this monster his friend.

"You look like you've seen a ghost," a familiar voice said behind him.

Mark turned slowly and saw the black-robed, skeletal figure coming toward him.

"So, you gave up being a griffin, Nimrod?"

Mark paused. "Or should I say Colonel Boggs?"

Boggs laughed. "It took you long enough to find out, not that it matters anymore. I should have figured out earlier that you had used the BioTel's virtual feedback loop to shut off Congo's BioBot. It was just my bad luck that the BioTels and the BioBots that Professor Rowberry used on Congo and the other lab animals operated on a different frequency than my MasterBot and BioBots."

"So that's why I couldn't read Red Rot and the Nanny's data signals the first time I was in the virtual loop," Mark said.

"And General Robbins' as well," Boggs nodded.

"So when R.J. expanded my BioTel's frequency range," Mark continued, "it let me tune into your BioBots."

"And let me to find you as well," Boggs said. "When I felt your signal interference, I simply followed it straight to you. The MasterBot also has a virtual feedback loop. After all, I was the one who had Professor Rowberry install the loop in the BioTel in the first place. Not that it matters to you, of course. Once I finish you off, I'll just turn on all the BioBots again and be back on schedule."

Mark had to change this madman's mind. "It's not the world's fault that you didn't get the promotion, Colonel. The Air Force might go easy on you, if you turn yourself in."

Boggs laughed again. "You mean life in prison, instead of the death penalty? No, I'll take my chances. If my plan works, General Robbins will go to prison for me, along with Red Rot and the Nanny. And I'll have millions in a secret Swiss bank account. Then, to top it off, I'll replace Robbins as commander of Vandenberg."

"You're crazy!" Mark said.

Boggs' eyes narrowed. "I deserved that promotion, not Robbins. Now they'll all pay! I never intended to hurt you or your friends, though. I was only using you to set up my cover story that Red Rot and the Nanny were carrying out General Robbins' orders."

Mark nodded. "I know. We read the report you put in the general's desk—the *fake* report."

"You're a clever one," Boggs said. "It's just your bad luck that you three boys came to the base instead of Professor Rowberry. I had to improvise when you showed up. I thought I'd gotten you out of the way when I left you in the cave above the aqueduct. Did you really think Red Rot tracked us there over solid rock? No, I had already told him where to go. Professor Rowberry would have stayed there, and I would have completed my plan. But you wouldn't stop trying to escape, and you wouldn't stop trying to save me. Rather ironic isn't it? Because you cared about me, you must die."

Mark edged away. Boggs' attack would come at any moment. "Just let me go. I won't say anything."

"It's too late for that," Boggs said. "Let's see what other ancient mythology I can remember. There's not enough room in here to fly, so I think I'll choose a creature that likes tunnels. How about a Minotaur?" His body shimmered as his muscles thickened and his head grew. Before Mark's eyes, a bull's head appeared on Boggs body. The Minotaur's huge horns spread across the entire tunnel. Boggs snorted, pawed the ground with his foot, and charged.

Mark turned and dashed down the twisting corridor, trying to get away from the snorting beast behind him. Desperate, Mark opened a memory door and leapt in.

He hit the ground in a cloud of sand on a hot, desert plain. F-16 jet fighters with U.S. Air Force markings screamed overhead. Wave after wave of the fighters attacked a column of tanks half a mile away. Exploding missiles rocked the ground, sending plumes of smoke and debris into the air. Mark caught a glimpse of an Iraqi flag on one of the tanks. Boggs had fought in the Gulf War.

Above him, the memory door shimmered.

Mark threw himself behind a sand dune as the Minotaur came though. "Where are you?" Boggs bellowed.

Mark stayed low and ran away behind the dune. Above him, he heard a primal shriek. He looked up and saw flashing claws racing out of the sun. Boggs had changed back into a griffin and was diving at him! Mark threw himself to the side, barely evading the talons. The griffin circled away, streaked through a plume of black smoke, and rose for another attack.

Mark had to do something fast. Becoming a lion-tamer wouldn't work again, Boggs was onto that. A sudden thought struck him: a lion-tamer couldn't defeat a monster like Boggs, but a monster-tamer might.

Destructo! His favorite comic book hero!

Mark heard the griffin's shriek again. He looked up and saw it fold its wings and dive!

Mark closed his eyes and formed a mental image of the tall, purple-suited hero with the red boots and swirling gold cloak. Mark envisioned the red Justice Stone around the super-hero's neck. Destructo's power emanated from the Justice Stone. Mark opened his mouth and chanted the words of power: "I am Destructo! As long as I am pure of heart and mind—I am invincible!"

Mark opened his eyes. "Justice Power!" he

yelled. A bolt of power shot from his arm and hit the griffin, bathing it in a red light. The blast threw the evil creature skyward. Then it became limp and fell toward the sand.

Loud clanking came from behind Mark. He whirled around and saw an Iraqi tank bearing down on him. He raised his hand and loosed another power bolt at the treads. The metal melted, stopping the tank. Moments later the turret swung toward Mark, and, with a belch of flame, the cannon fired.

"Mirror shield on!" Mark commanded. A field of red energy shimmered in front of him. The shell hit the shield, reversed direction, and sped back toward the tank. The mirror shield had reflected the weapon back on its source.

The shell burst into flames with a deafening roar, rocking the tank back and forth. The top hatch flipped open, and the tank commander and two enlisted men scrambled out.

"Retreat!" The tank commander yelled. "Superman is real! He's on the American's side!"

"Not Superman!" Mark yelled at the retreating figures. "Destructo!"

He had to get back to Red Storm and save his friends. "Power up!" he commanded. He rose into the air, flew toward the open memory door, and passed into the tunnel. Mark looked around trying to remember the way out.

"Not so fast!" Boggs yelled from behind. "There are more powerful creatures in mythology than the griffin!"

Boggs was still alive!

Mark looked through the doorway and saw a shimmering figure in a white toga floating above the sand. A green wreath lay on his head and sparks flew from his eyes. "Have you never heard of Zeus, Lord of Olympus?" he yelled. The figure put his arm up, and a bolt of lightning appeared in his hand. With a sudden motion, he flung the crackling bolt at Mark. "Die, mortal!"

Mark crossed his arm in front of him. "Mirror shield on!"

The lightning bolt hit the red energy field and reflected back at an angle. It hit the open memory door and slammed it shut, melting it into the wall until no door remained. Only the small window was left in the twisted wreckage. Mark stepped forward and looked through it. Boggs now looked like himself, about fifty years old, short, muscular, and with panic on his face. He beat against the window with his fists.

"Don't leave me trapped in my own memories!" he cried. "Let me out! Don't leave me like this!"

Mark tugged at the door, but it wouldn't budge.

"I can't open it!" Mark yelled. "You've damaged the brain tissue somehow, and that part of your memory is cut off. If I try to blast you out, I might cause more damage and kill you. I can't risk it." Mark stepped back.

"No!" Boggs screamed. "Come back!"

"Power on," Mark ordered. With Destructo's power at his command, Mark glided out of Boggs' mind and into the MasterBot exit channel. He stepped into the data return stream. In moments he was back on the CPU obelisk.

He saw the two logic gates that controlled the link to Boggs' MasterBot. He didn't hesitate. Grabbing both gates securely, he slammed them shut. As Mark's vision blurred, signaling his return to the real world, he thought about Colonel Boggs. Once an honorable man, Boggs had let pride ruin his life. Now he was lost forever— trapped in the wreckage of his own mad brain.

MegaBlast

Mark's vision cleared, and he found himself in Red Storm's missile room again, floating behind the rotary launcher. Mark saw Red Rot and the Nanny floating in front of him. The blow gun was still in her hand but she was limp, and her eyes were closed. Red Rot's eyes were closed too.

Mark pushed off the launcher and floated to the main part of the room.

"Oh, man," Blue said by the far wall, "do I have a headache!"

R.J. was next to him. He saw Mark. "Was it my imagination, or was I just trying to kill you?"

"The Nanny darted you," Mark said. "I had to go back inside the BioTel and shut off your BioBot."

"Look out, Harrison!" Blue screamed.

Mark whirled around and saw Red Rot and the Nanny coming toward him. They had regained consciousness.

Blue pushed off the wall and flew past Mark. "I'll get 'em!"

"No, Blue!" Mark yelled. "Don't hurt them!"

Red Rot became alarmed. "Yes, please don't . . ." His words were cut off as Blue put him in a headlock.

"I'll pound 'em!" Blue yelled. He reached for the Nanny, but she evaded his hand.

"Please, young man," she cried. "We're not your enemies."

"She's right, Blue!" Mark hollered. "They were controlled by Nimrod!"

Blue stopped wrenching Red Rot's head. "What?"

"You can let Red Rot go," Mark said. "Nimrod injected them both with BioBots."

R.J. floated over to Mark. "You mean General Robbins was controlling them?"

Mark shook his head. "No, Colonel Boggs."

R.J. looked confused. "Boggs is Nimrod?"

Mark shook his head again. "*Was* Nimrod. He's not going to be anything anymore—except maybe a vegetable."

Blue let Red Rot go. "I don't get any of this, Harrison. Our friends are our enemies now, and our enemies are our friends?"

"I'll explain later," Mark said. He looked at Red Rot. "Are you okay?"

"I believe so," the tall, thin man said, rubbing

his neck, "but your friend has quite a grip." He looked at Blue. "Have you considered a career as a field operative?"

Blue looked offended. "I ain't gonna be a doctor and operate in fields. Doctors gotta wear them wimpy-lookin' robes." He thought for a moment. "'Course they do get to play with knives."

"Do you two know where you are?" Mark asked.

"Yes," the Nanny replied, floating next to Red Rot, "aboard Red Storm. We nearly committed the perfect crime—against our will. Now, we must exit the station before it explodes."

Mark had a plan. "Let's radio for a rescue crew," he suggested. "With Boggs out of commission, we don't have a shuttle pilot anymore."

Red Rot shook his head. "There's no time for a rescue. The timer on the nuclear warhead is set to go off in twenty minutes."

R.J. seemed surprised. "What timer? We thought you were going to set it off remotely."

"No," Red Rot answered. "Boggs didn't want to risk the detonation signal being jammed. The timer's running right now."

"So you were going to help Boggs blow up Red Storm and a billion dollar space shuttle?" Blue asked.

The Nanny nodded. "We would have done

anything under Boggs' control. But he was going to kill us, too, when we got back to earth." She faced Mark. "We saw your battle with Boggs through the BioBot input channel."

Mark nodded. "I was only able to turn off the output channels on three of the BioBots. You must have seen the whole fight."

"What fight?" R.J. asked. "I saw nothing."

"Me neither," Blue added, looking disappointed. "Harrison finally beats somebody up and I miss it."

"Both of your BioBots must have gotten turned off before the battle," the Nanny said. "Take my word for it. Mark saved your lives. He saved all our lives. He's a hero."

"We're not saved yet," Mark said. "We still have to figure out a way to shut off the nuclear warhead's timer."

Red Rot shook his head. "The controls are in the *Explorer's* main cabin, where Boggs is, and he's locked it from the inside. There's no way in."

Mark thought. There *had* to be a way out of this. "What about the escape pod?" he asked.

Again Red Rot shook his head. "Not only is it filled with five nuclear warheads, but only Boggs knows how to fly it."

"We were hoping it had an autopilot," Mark said.

"I'm afraid not," Red Rot said. "The CIA figured that anyone up here would already be trained to fly it."

"So we just wait for the bomb to go off?" Blue asked in frustration.

"No," Mark said. "We came this far and we're not giving up. Let's get to the escape pod."

"But we can't fly it," R.J. said. "You heard Sir Rottingham."

"That's right," Mark said, "we can't, but General Robbins can. He's a certified shuttle pilot. I saw it in Boggs' memory."

"What are you talkin' about?" Blue said. "Boggs ain't here!"

"No, but he can be," Mark said. "I shut off *five* BioBots inside the BioTel's computer. There's only four of you here, so Robbins had to be the fifth. Maybe we can link with him again."

"What? . . ." Blue started.

"Let's just get to the pod," Mark said. "You'll have to trust me." Mark hoped he knew what he was doing.

"You've done pretty well so far," Red Rot said. "Follow me."

Under Red Rot's direction they exited the missile room, floated down a long corridor, and entered a large, white docking station. A small round hatch was open to another room.

"The escape pod is through that door," Red Rot

said. "It's connected to the outside of the station, and it's ready to go—except for the warheads."

"Hurry!" Mark said. "Let's get them out!"

"They're harmless unless they're armed," the Nanny said. "Leave them in the cargo bay. We don't have time to remove them."

"You're right," Mark said. "Everyone in. We only have a few minutes left!"

Mark went to the front of the small cockpit and keyed the radio transmitter. "Red Storm to Vandenberg, Red Storm to Vandenberg, please come in. We must speak to General Robbins."

A voice crackled over the radio. "Who is this? This is a restricted frequency. You are not authorized to . . ."

"Never mind that," Mark said. "We're on Red Storm, and the station is going to blow. Get General Robbins immediately."

There was a long pause then General Robbins came on. "Red Storm? Who the devil is this? I snapped out of Colonel Boggs' BioBot control thirty minutes ago. All of his men have been rounded up." He paused. "Is this the boy I saw through my BioBot link?"

"Yes, General, it is," Mark said. "We've got a problem here. A nuclear warhead on Red Storm is set to blow in a few minutes, and we're in the escape pod trying to get away. The problem is, none of us knows how to fly it."

There was a long pause. "I can't help you," General Robbins finally said. "The controls are too complicated to talk you down."

"You *can* help us, General," Mark said. "Go to the storage room in the Command Bunker where the aqueduct inspection hatch is. There's a row of lockers on one wall. In one of the lockers I left a plastic case containing a BioTel which I want you to put on. I'll have the Nanny dart me. Then I want you to radio up the BioTel's signal. You can fly the shuttle through me."

"It just might work," Robbins said. "I'll use a tight-beam microwave frequency to relay the BioTel signal. That way, no one can interrupt it. I'm on my way."

Mark turned to the Nanny. "Dart me."

She shook her head. "You're a very brave lad, but I've piloted jet fighters before. I can better stand the G-forces." Taking a case from her suit, she loaded a BioBot into the hollow tube and blew the dart into her arm.

"Wait!" Mark said.

"She's stubborn when she's right," Red Rot said. "Let's get her into the pilot's chair."

Mark helped buckle her in.

The Nanny shuddered slightly and then spoke, a sharp tone of command in her voice. "This is incredible! I'm actually here!" The general had linked up with her.

"What do we do?" Mark asked.

"Prepare to undock," the Nanny barked. "All crew members secure yourselves." Like a concert pianist, the Nanny's fingers flew over the instrument panel with lightning speed. She released the craft from Red Storm and fired the maneuvering jets. The small spacecraft slowly backed away.

Another voice came over the radio. "What's going on? Who's in the escape pod?"

It was Boggs' voice.

Mark was momentarily confused. How had the colonel escaped?

"Clearing Red Storm," the Nanny said.

"Minnifield, is that you?" Boggs asked. "You must obey my orders!"

"She won't listen to you," Mark said into the radio. "General Robbins is beaming a high-power BioTel signal into her BioBot from Earth. Your MasterBot signal can't override it."

"No!" Boggs screamed.

"How'd you get out of the memory you were trapped in?" Mark said.

"Memories are interlaced," Boggs replied. "I simply found another memory door. Apparently, it took too long."

"Long enough for me to take your men at Vandenberg prisoner," the Nanny said. Mark realized that General Robbins was speaking through her. "You were a good man, Boggs," the general continued in the Nanny's voice, "but you're finished now. I'll bring you to justice if I have to commit the full weight of the United States military!"

The Nanny's hands continued to fly over the instrument panel. Mark was fascinated. Linked with General Robbins, the Nanny was flying the escape module like an expert.

Boggs' voice rose in anger. "Perhaps you have forgotten that I can disable the timer from here and re-target the missile in the rotary launcher. And Red Storm's targeting radar is the most accurate ever made. And remember, I can still fly the space shuttle. With you out of the way, I'll fly it to earth, land in a terrorist country, and sell the *Explorer* to the highest bidder. I'm not finished, but you are. I may not ever become commander of Vandenberg, but I'll still be very rich."

"Hurry!" Blue urged the Nanny.

The Nanny pushed several more buttons, and the escape pod began slowly accelerating.

"Ready to launch," Boggs said with a chuckle. "Preparing to target the escape pod."

"Get us out of here!" Mark said.

"We're still under maneuvering jets," the Nanny said. "If I start the engines too early, we'll launch into space and never be able to get back to earth."

"Glad to see you all know you're going to die," Boggs said. "I'm sorry, but I must be going now. I have friends waiting for me."

Mark held his breath as they crawled away from the space station.

"Main engines engaging now!" the Nanny said. With a smooth rush of acceleration, the little vehicle blasted away. A buzzer went off in the cabin.

"Electromagnetic pulse detected by sensors," the Nanny reported. "It's a targeting radar. Boggs has got us."

Blue moaned, and Mark closed his eyes. They had come so close to succeeding, but now it was over.

Boggs's voice came over the radio again. "You're all dead, but I, on the other hand, am going to get everything I have coming to me."

R.J. spoke softly. "I suspect you will, Colonel. You'll get everything you deserve."

"Good-bye, all," Boggs said.

There was a short pause and everyone held their breath. Boggs' voice came over the radio again. "This is strange," he said quickly, "the readout says the launch port has opened, but I just felt a shock like something had closed. I have to abort." Boggs paused then spoke again. "I can't stop the launch! It's gone past fail-safe!"

"It's like you said," R.J. uttered. "You're getting everything you deserve."

"What did you do?" Boggs cried.

"When we came in through the missile tube," R.J. continued, "I rewired the controls. I changed it so that the command to close the tube would make it open, and the command to open it would make it close. Your live missile is stuck in the missile tube."

"No!" Boggs screamed.

The radio went dead, and a brilliant explosion of pure energy suddenly lit the darkness of space. Mark shielded his eyes as Red Storm instantly evaporated in a million degrees of nuclear heat. A shock wave from the megablast rocked the escape pod, but the craft had pulled far enough away to escape severe damage.

Moments later the flash disappeared and the blackness of space returned.

"You did it, Fatberry!" Blue screamed. "You saved us!"

"You three boys are full of surprises," the general said through the Nanny.

R.J. sat in his seat beaming.

As Mark watched the earth growing in the screen, he wondered about the trick R.J. had played on Boggs. "Why didn't you tell us about the missile tube, R.J.?" he asked. "We thought we were going to die."

R.J. looked somberly at Mark. "Because of Blue."

"What?" Blue said, appearing puzzled.

"If it didn't work," R.J. explained, "I didn't want Blue to have an excuse to ridicule me."

Blue shook his head. "I don't get it. Since when do I need an excuse to make fun of you?"

The three boys looked at each other then broke into laughter.

Destructo

Mark sat on his bed and opened the newest issue of *Destructo the Monster-Tamer*. It had been three weeks since they had returned from space, and Mark was trying to fit into his normal routine. Upon landing at Vandenberg, they'd spent two days being debriefed by the CIA, NASA, the U.S. Air Force, and the British Secret Service.

The three boys had agreed to keep silent about their ordeal. If the world were to learn about Red Storm or discover that the United States had nearly lost five nuclear warheads, the United Nations might collapse from distrust of its most powerful member—America. In exchange for his silence, however, Mark had insisted that Congo and the other animals in the lab be given homes at the San Diego Wild Animal Park. The Air Force eagerly agreed, realizing they'd gotten off easy.

R.J. and Blue, however, had taken more convincing. R.J. had wanted to make money from the publicity, and Blue had wanted to sell his story to Hollywood. It had taken a call from Professor Rowberry to quiet R.J., and a personal conversation with Andre. K. Brockman, the President of the United States, to silence Blue.

On Mark's testimony, Sir Redford Rottingham, alias Red Rot, had been cleared of all charges and been given a promotion to head MI-5's Space Intelligence Division in London. Mrs. Minerva Minnifield, the Nanny, had received a personal commendation from the Queen. She was now Chief of Security for England's Royal Family at Buckingham Palace. Before parting, she had made Mark, Blue, and R.J. promise to visit England someday as her personal guests.

General Robbins, though, no longer commanded Vandenberg. He had been promoted to the Joint Chiefs of Staff and sent to the Pentagon outside Washington, D.C. Ironically, that move had been planned months ago. The man who would have been promoted to Commander at Vandenberg was Colonel Boggs. If only Boggs could have waited and gone through proper channels, he would have gotten his wish.

Mark's stomach growled with hunger. He reached under his bed for his granola box, but his hand hit something else. He looked down and saw a pile of old spit wads. Since Clint's back-yard campout three weeks ago, Mark had been finding spit wads everywhere. He threw the pile into his wastebasket. As dangerous as facing Nimrod had been, at least Mark had missed Clint's campout. He would rather fight ten men like Colonel Boggs, any day, than face a pack of spit wad-shooting Cub Scouts.

Mark grabbed the granola box and opened it. Instead of the luscious Ding-Dongs he'd expected to find, though, he saw a pile of revolting nut-date granola. A note lay on top:

"Mark, I thought you'd like your granola box to be filled with real granola. I threw all the junk food away. Love, Mom."

Mark dropped the box, a half-smile on his face. She was clever, that mom of his. He'd have to change his hiding place again. Never mind, though, Joe's Market was close by, and there'd be other days and other Ding-Dongs. His mom may have won the battle, but she hadn't won the war.

Mark flopped onto his bed to read *Destructo*. This issue was titled "Slave Merchants from Dimension X."

Ha! Mark thought. The merchants wouldn't stand a chance against Destructo's Justice Stone. He remembered his fight with Nimrod on the desert battlefield. The Justice Stone had defeated creatures far deadlier than Dimension X slavers.

Mark looked up and stared out his window. What if he hadn't developed his imagination by reading *Destructo?* He might have been killed by Boggs. He had tried to tell R.J. and Blue about the battle, but they didn't understand how real it had been, so he quit trying. It didn't matter that they didn't know how Destructo had saved them. Mark knew, though, and that was enough. He opened the first page.

Destructo the Monster-Tamer, Defender of the Galaxy and Master of the Universe, sat at the controls of his Peace Cruiser. He gazed at the Martian landscape passing serenely beneath him. Having completed his weekly patrol of the Solar System, he prepared to head back to Justice Mountain on Earth. Suddenly his Justice Stone flared bright red—a distress message was coming in!

"This is Phobos Station! We are under attack from the Slave Merchants! Request immediate assistance . . ." The message cut out, leaving only static.

Destructo rubbed his Justice Stone, and a fierce look came into his

*eyes. "The Dimension X evildoers will
not prevail! I am Destructo! As long as
I am pure of heart and mind, I am
invincible!" The Peace Cruiser's
hyperjets kicked in, and Destructo
wheeled the craft into a tight turn
toward Phobos. He smiled grimly—he
had a date with destiny.*

The doorbell rang, jerking Mark back from
Mars. "Clint! Get that!"

"You get it!" Clint yelled back. "I'm watchin'
the Sludge Mutants!"

"Answer the door or I won't let you read this
month's *Destructo*!" Mark threatened. "It came
today!"

Clint paused a moment. "Okay! I'm gettin'
it."

Mark smiled. Destructo was always good for
occasionally blackmailing Clint. Moments later
his bedroom door swung open and R.J. and Blue
entered. Mark sat up.

Blue sat on Mark's desk. "Me and R.J. are
headin' over to the Chip Factory. They got a new
video game there—*Space Shuttle Pilot*. I figure
with all my experience I'm a cinch for the top
score."

R.J. winced. "I'm not wasting my time with
mere video games. They recently began selling

whole-wheat, chocolate chip cookies. I thought I'd try one or two."

"More like one or two hundred," Blue scoffed. "You wanna come, Harrison?"

Mark thought about it. "I'm busy now. Why don't I meet you there in a half-hour or so?"

R.J. saw the magazine in Mark's hand. "A comic book? Mark, haven't you outgrown those by now?"

Blue's shivered. "Just the thought of readin' gives me the creeps." Blue slid off the desk and took a step toward the bed. "In fact, I outta take that thing and . . ."

A low growl came from beneath Mark's bed, and a small, amber-colored poodle with a red ribbon in each ear stalked out.

Blue froze. "I didn't know Miss Fluffy was in here."

Miss Fluffy's mouth was too small to grab necks, so she went for ears. And like the pit bull she thought she was, once she latched on, she never let go.

"C'mon, Harrison," Blue pleaded, "call her off." He backed against the wall and put a hand on each side of his head. "I'll treat you to a game of *Shuttle Pilot*."

"It's okay, girl," Mark said. "Come here." The tiny poodle turned and jumped onto the bed.

"That comic ain't worth dyin' over," Blue

said, keeping an eye on Miss Fluffy. "But I still don't know why you like 'em so much."

Mark wished Blue and R.J. could understand that every time he read *Destructo* he saw himself cruising the far-off reaches of the galaxy, warping to distant stars, and saving humanity. But he knew it was useless to explain it again. "I don't know why I like comics so much either. I guess it's just a good way to kill time."

"Or your brain cells," R.J. said. "Let's go, Blue. If we delay, all the cookies might be gone."

They will be for sure after you get there," Blue said. "See ya in a bit, Harrison. Leave Dogzilla here, huh?" They turned and walked out under Miss Fluffy's watchful gaze.

Glad to be alone, Mark leaned back on the bed and opened the comic. Within seconds he was above Mars again, racing toward Phobos to fight the slavers from Dimension X. Things looked bad now, but he knew justice would prevail.

After all, Destructo was on the way, and Destructo never lost.